CBSE

[Central Board of Secondary Education]

ACCOUNTANCY

CLASS - XII

Content Table

Chapter- 1   Accounting for Partnership Firms

Introduction

"Partnership is the relations between two or more persons who have agreed to share the profits of a business carried on by all or any one of them acting for all".

Features of Partnership

The following are the five features of a partnership:

1.   Two or more persons
There must be at least two persons to form a valid partnership. The maximum number of partners cannot exceed the number of partners prescribed by Companies Act, 2013 which is 50 in any business whether banking or non- banking.

2.   Agreement
Partnership comes into existence by an agreement (either written or oral among the partners. The written agreement among the partners is called Partnership Deed.

3.   Existence of business and profit motive
A partnership can be formed for the purpose of carrying on legal business with the intention of earning profits. A joint ownership of some property by itself cannot be called a partnership.

4.   Sharing of Profits
An agreement between the partners must be aimed at sharing the profits. If some persons join hands to run some charitable activity, it will not be called partnership. Futher, if a partner is deprived of his right to share the profits of the business, he cannot be called as partner.

5.   Buiness carried on by all or any of them acting for all
It means that each partner can participate in the conduct of business and each partner is bound by the acts of other partners in respect to the business of the firm.

Partnership Deed

Since partnership is the outcome of an agreement, it is essential that there must be some terms and conditions agreed upon by all the partners. Such terms and conditions mat be either written or oral. The law does not make it compulsory to have a written agreement. However, in order to avoid all misunderstandings and disputes, it is always the best course to have a written agreement duly signed and registered under the Act.

The partnership deed is a written agreement among the partners which contains the terms of agreement. It is also called 'Articles of Partnership'. A partnership deed should contain the following points:
* Name and address of the firm as well as partners.
* Name and addresses of the partners.
* Nature and place of the business.
* Duration, if any of partnership.
* Capital contribution by each partner.
* Interest on capital.
* Drawings and interest on drawings.
* Profit sharing ratio.
* Interest on loan.
* Partner's Salary/commission etc.
* Method for valuation of goodwill and assets.
* Accounting period of the firm and duration of partnership
* Rights and duties of partners how disputes will be settled.
* Decisions taken if some partner becomes insolvent.

- Opening of Bank Account – whereas it will be in the name of firm or partners.
- Rules to be followed in case of admission & Settlement of accounts or retirement or death of partner.
- Revaluation of assets & liabilities, if any to be done.
- Method of recording of firm's accounts
- Auditing
- Date of commencement of partnership

Benefits of Partnership Deed

- It regulates the rights, duties and liabilites of each partner.
- It helps to avoid any misunderstanding amongst the partners because all the terms and conditins of partnership have been laid down beforehand in the deed.
- Any dispute amongst the partners may be settled easily as the partnership deed may be readiy referred to.

Rules applicable in the absence of partnership deed

Profit sharing Ratio	Equal, Irrespective of capital contribution.
Interest on Capital	No Interest on Capital is to be allowed to any Partner
Interest on Drawings	No interest on Drawings is to be charged to any partner
Salary or Commission to a Partner	Not allowed to any partner
Interest on loan by a Partner	Interest is allowed @ 6% per annum.

Provision of Partnership Act 1932 in the Absence of Partnership Deed

In the absence of a partnership deed, the following accounting rules apply:

A partnership deed includes all matters regarding the partners' mutual relationships. The accounting shall be conducted in accordance with the following provisions of the Indian Partnership Act of 1932, in the absence of an agreement.

Interest on Capital: Partners cannot earn interest on their capital. When there is a profit, interest is only paid if it is allowed by the partnership agreement. Interest is not paid in case of loss.

Interest on Drawings: The partners will not be charged interest on drawings they make.

Salary/ Commission to Partner: Unless otherwise provided in the partnership agreement, partners are not entitled to salary/ commission.

Interest on Loan: Each of the firm's partners is entitled to six per cent interest on advancing money to the firm (as opposed to just his share capital).

Profit-sharing Ratio: Every partner of the firm receives an equal share of the profits regardless of how much capital they contribute.

Partner's Capital Accounts

Partner's Capital Accounts is an account which represents the partners interest in the business.

In case of partnership business, a separate capital account is mainted for each partner. The capital accounts of partners may be maintained by any of the following two methods.

1. Fixed Capital Accounts
2. Fluctuating Capital Accounts

1.   Fixed Capital Accounts

Under this method the original capitals invested by the partners remain constant, unless additional capital is introduced by an agreement. All entries relating to drawings, interest on capitals, interest on drawings, salary to partner, share of profits/losses are made in separate account whihc is called as Current Account. Thus the following two accounts are maintained when capitals are fixed.

- **Capital Account**

This account will always show a credit balance: Balance of Capital account remains fixed, it does not change every year that is why it is called fixed capital method.

Partner's Capital A/Cs

Particulars	X(Rs.)	Y(Rs.)	Particulars	X(Rs.)	Y(Rs.)
To Cash/Bank A/c (Capital Withdrawn)			By Balance b/d (Opening Cr. Balance)		
To Balance c/d (Closing balance)			By Cash/Bank A/c (Additional Capital Introduced)		

- **Current Account**

The Current account may show a debit or credit balance. All the usual adjustments such as interest on Capital, partner's salary/commission, drawings (out of profits), interest on drawings and share in profits or losses etc. are recorded in this account.All the Current Year's adjustments are recorded in this account, that is why it is called Current account.

Partner's Current A/Cs

Particulars	X(Rs.)	Y(Rs.)	Particulars	X(Rs.)	Y(Rs.)
To Balance b/d (Opening Dr. Balance)			By Balance b/d (Opening Cr. Balance)		
To Drawings (out of Profits)			By Interest on Capital		
To Interest on Drawings			By Partner's Salary or Commission		
To Profit and Loss A/c (Share in losses)			By Profit and Loss Appropriation A/c (Share in Profits)		
To Balance c/d (Closing credit Balance)			By Balance c/d (Closing Dr. Balance)		

2. Fluctuating Capital Accounts

In this method only one account i.e., Capital Account of each and every partner is prepared and all the adjustment such as interest on capital interest on drawings etc, are recorded in this account under this method, Capital account may show a debit or credit balance and the balance of this account changes frequently from time to time therefore it is called fluctuating Capital Account.In this method the capitals are not fixed. In the absence of information, the Capital Accounts should be prepared by this method.

Partner's Capital

Particulars	X(Rs.)	Y(Rs.)	Particulars	X(Rs.)	Y(Rs.)
To Balance b/d (Opening Dr. Balance)			By Balance b/d (Opening Cr. Balance)		
To Cash/Bank A/c (Capital Withdrawn)			By Cash/Bank A/c (Additional Capital Introduced)		
To Drawings (out of profits)			By Interest on Capital		
To Interest on Drawings			By Partner's Salary or Commission		
To Profit and Loss A/c (Share in losses)			By Profit and Loss Appropriation A/c (Share in Profits)		
To Balance c/d (Closing credit Balance)			By Balance c/d (Closing Dr. Balance)		

Transactiions of the partnerhsip firm are recorded according to the principles of Double-entry book keeping system, and as in the case of a sole proprietorship concern a partnership firm will also prepare Trading account, Profit & Loss account and Balance Sheet at the end of every year. The only difference between accounting of a sole trader and partnership firm is that the profits of the partnership firm ar divided amongst the partners.

A Profit and Loss Appropriation Account is prepared to show the distribution of profits among partners as per the provision of Partnership Deed (or as per the provision of Indian Partnership Act, 1932 in the absence of Partnership Deed). It is an extension of profit and Loss Account. It is nominal account. It records entries for interest on capital, Interest on Drawings, Salary to the partner, and division of profits among the partners.

The Journal Entries regarding Profit and Loss Appropriation Account are as follows:

1. For transfer of balance of Profit and Loss Account
Profit and Loss A/c Dr.
To Profit and Loss Appropriation A/c

2. For Interest on Capital
For allowing Interest on capital

- **Interest on Capital A/c**
To Partner's Capital/Current A/c's
(Being interest on capital allowed @ % p.a.)

- **For transferring Interest on Capital to p&L appropriation A/c.**
Profit and Loss Appropriation A/c Dr.
To Interest on Capital A/c.
(Being interest on capital transferred to p&L Appropriation A/c)

3. For Salary or Commission payable to a partner
- **For allowing Salary or Commission to a partner:**
Partners Salary/Commission A/c Dr.
To Partner's Capital/Current A/c's
(Being salary/commission payable to a partner)

- **For transferring Partner's Salary/Commission A/c to Profit and Loss**
Appropriation A/s:
Profit and Loss Appropriation A/c Dr.
To Partner's Salary/Commission A/c

4. For transfer of Reserves
Profit and Loss Appropriation A/c Dr.
To Reserve A/c
(Being reserve created)

5. For Interest on Drawings
- For charging interest on a **partner's** drawings:
Partner's Capital/Current A/c   ` Dr.
To Interest on Drawings A/c
(Being interest on drawings charged @ % p.a.)

- For transferring interest on drawings to Profit and Loss **Appropriation** A/c
Interest on Drawings A/c Dr.
To Profit and Loss Appropriation A/c
(Being interest on drawings transferred to P&L appropriation A/c)

6. For transfer to Profit (i.e. Credit Balance of Profit and Loss Appropriation Account

Profit and Loss Appropriation A/c Dr.

To Partners Capital/Current A/cs

(Being profits distributed among partners)

Guarantee of Profits to a Partner

Guarantee is an assurance given to the partner of the firm that at least a fixed amount shall be given to him/her irrespective of his/her actual share in profits of the firm. If actual share in profits is less than the guaranteed amount in that case the deficit amount shall be borne either by the firm or by any partner as the case may be or as may have been decided by ana agreement.

Guarantee to a partner is given for minimum share in profits. If the actual share in profits is more than the minimum share in profits, then the actual profits will be allowed to the partner.

Case: 1. When guarantee is given by FIRM (i.e. by all the Partners of the firm)

- If share in actual profits is less than the guaranteed amount then. Guaranteed amount to a partner is first written off against the profits and then,
- Remaining profits are distributed among the remaining partners in the remaining ratio.

Case: 2. When guarantee is given by a partner or partners to another partner.

- Calculate the share in profits for the partner to whom guarantee is given.
- If share in profits is more than the guaranteed amount, distribute the profit as per the profit and loss sharing ratio in usual manner.
- If share in profits is less than the guaranteed amount, find the difference between the share in profits and the guaranteed amount and the difference known as deficiency.

Deficiency is contributed by the partner or partners who guaranteed in certain ratio and subtracted from his or their respective shares.

Past Adjustments

If, after preparation of Final Accounts of firm, it is found that some errors or commission in accounts has occurred than such errors or omissions are rectified in the next year by passing an adjustment entry.

A statement is prepared to ascertain the net effect of such errors or omissions on partner's capital/current accounts in the following manner.

Statement showing adjustment

Particulars	A (Rs.)	B (Rs.)	C (Rs.)
A Amount to be given credited			
Interest on Capital			
(Not allowed or provided at a lower rate)			
Partner's Salary or Commission etc.			
(Omitted to be recorded)			
Actual Profits			
(To be distributed in correct ratio)			
Total A			
B. Amount already given to be taken back now debited			
+ Interest on Capital			
(If given at a higher rate)			

+ Interest on Drawings			
(If not charged)			
+ Profits already distributed in wrong ratio			
(debited now)			
Total B			
Net Effect (A-B)	+/-	+/-	+/-

+ Indicates Amount to be Credited to Partner's Capital Account – Indicates Amount to be Debited to Partners Capital Account

Journal

Date	Particulars	LF.	Debit(Rs.)	Debit(Rs.)
	Partners Capital A/C Dr.			
	(Amount to be Debited)			
	To Partners' Capital A/c			
	(Amount to be Credited)			
	(Being adjustment entry passed)			

During Past Adjustment it is not compulsory that capital accounts of all partners are affected. More than one partners Capital Account may be debited or credited but amount of debit & credit should be equal.

Goodwill

Goodwill is good name or the reputaion of the business, which is earned by a firm through the hardwork and honesty of its owners. If a firm renders good service to the customers, the customers who feel satisfied will come again and aain and the firm will be able to earn more profits in future.

Thus, goodwill is the value of the reputaion of a firm which enables it to earn higher profits in comparison to the normal profits earned by other firms in the same trade.

Features of Goodwill

- **It is an intangible asset:** Goodwill cannot be seen or touched, it does not have any physical existence, thus it belongs to the category of intangible assets such as patents, trademarks, copyrights, etc.
- **It is a valuable asset:** Goodwill is an valuable asset that accounts for the excess purchase price of another company. Items included in goodwill are proprietary or intellectual property and brand recognition, which are not easily quantifiable.
- **It is helpful in earning excess profits:** Goodwill is the value of the reputaion of a firm which enables it to earn higher profits in comparison to the normal profits earned by other firms in the same trade.
- **Its value is liable to constant fluctuations:** While goodwill does not depreciate, its value is liable to constant fluctuation, its vlaue is liable to constant fluctuations.It is always present as a silent asset in a business where there are super profits (i.e.more than the normal) but declines in value with the decline in earnings.
- **It is valuable only when entire business is sold:** Goodwill cannot be sold in part. It can be sold with the entire business only. The only exception is at the time of admission or retirement of the partner.
- **It is difficult to place an exact value on goodwill:** This is beecause its value may fluctuate from time to time due to changing circumsatnces which are internat and external to business.

Categories of Goodwill

Goodwill is divided into two categories. They are:

1. Purchased Goodwill

Purchased goodwill means goodwill for which a consideration has been paid e.g. when business is purchased the excess of purchase consideration of its net assets i.e. (Assets – Liabilities) is the Purchased Goodwill. It is separately recorded in the books because as it is purchased by paying in form of cash or kind.

2. Self-generated Goodwill

Self-generated Goodwill also called as inherent goodwill. It is an internally generated goodwill which arises from a number of factors that a running business possesses due to which it is able to earn more profits in the future.

Factors Affecting the Value of Goodwill

1. Efficient management
If the business is run by experienced and efficient management, its profits will go on increasing, which results in increase in the value of goodwill.

2. Quality of products
If the firm is suppyong good quality of products, then the customer will come again and again for the same and thus will create the goodwill and brand name for the same.

3. Location of business
If the business is located at a convenient or prominent place, it will atract more customers and therefore will have more goodwill.

4. The Longevity of the business
An older business is better known to its customers, therefore it is likely to have more goodwill. When a business enterprise has built up good repuation over a period of time, the number of customers will be more in comparison to the customers of new entrants. Number of customers is an indicator of profit earning capacity of a business.

5. Monopolistic and other Rights
If a buiness enjoys monopoly market, it will have assured profits. Similarly, if it holds some special rights such as patents, trade marks, copyrights or concessions, etc, it will have more goodwill.

6. Other factors
- Good industrial relations.
- Favourable Government regulations
- Stable political conditions
- Research and development efforts
- Effective advertising to establish brand popularity
- Popularity of product in terms of quality.

Mutual rights change under following circumstances
- When profit sharing ratio changes
- On admission of a partner
- On Retirement or death of a partner
- When amalgamation of two firms taken place
- When partnership firm is sold.

Method of valuation of goodwill
It is very difficult to assess the value of goodwill, as it is an intangible asset. In case of sale of a business, its value depends on the mutual agreement between the seller and the purchaser of the business. Usually, there are three methods of valuing goodwill:

1. Average profit method
This method is divided into two sub-division.
- **Simple Average:** In this process, goodwill evaluation is done by calculating the average profit by the number of years it is called years purchase. It can be calculated by using the formula. Goodwill = Average Profit x No. of years' of purchase.
- **Weighted Average:** Here, last year's profit is calculated by a specific number of weights. It is used to obtain the value of goods, which is divided by the total number of weights for determining the average weight profit. This technique is used when there is a change in profits and giving high importance to the present year's profit. It is evaluated by using the formula. Goodwill = Weighted Average Profit x No. of years' of purchase, where Weighted Average Profit = Sum of Profits multiplied by weights/ Sum of weights.

2. Super profit method
It is a surplus of expected future maintainable profits over normal profits. The two methods of these methods are:

- **The Purchase Method by Number of Years:** The goodwill is established by evaluating super-profits by a specific number of the purchase year. It can be estimated by applying the below formula. Super Profit = Actual or Average profit – Normal Profit.
- **Annuity Method:** Here, the average super profit is taken as an annuity value over a definite number of years. A discounted amount of super profit calculates the current value of an annuity at the given rate of interest. The formula to be used here is Goodwill = Super Profit × Discounting Factor.

3. **Capitalization method**

Under this method, goodwill can be evaluated by two methods.
- **Average Profits Method:** In this process, goodwill is measured by subtracting the original capital applied from the capitalised amount of the average profits based on the average return rate. The formula is Capitalised Average profits = Average Profits × (100/average return rate)
- **Super Profits Method:** Here, the super profit is capitalised, and the goodwill is calculated. The formula applied is Goodwill = Super Profits × (100/ Normal Rate of Return)

Chance in Profit Sharing Ratio Among the Existing Partners

Meaning of Reconstruction

Any change in agreement of partnership or profit sharing ratio is called reconstitution of partnership firm. In following circumstances a partnership firm may be reconstituted:
1. Change in Profit Sharing Ratio
2. Admission of a partner
3. Retirement/Death of a partner

A Change in profit sharing ratio means one or more partners acquires interest form another partner or partners. Here it share of profit of one or more partners increases then share of one or more partner decreases to same extent.

New profit sharing ratio

The ratio in which the partners are to share the profits in future on reconstitution is known as New profit sharing ratio.

Gaining Ratio

It is the ratio in which the profit sharing ratio of gaining partners increases. It is calculated by taking difference between New profit sharing ratio and old profit sharing ratio.

Sacrificing Ratio

It is the ratio in which the profit sharing ratio of sacrificing partners decreases. It is calculated by taking difference between old profit sharing ratio and new profit sharing ratio.

Accounting Treatment of Goodwill

In case of change in profit sharing ratio, the gaining partner must components the sacrificing partner by paying the proportionate amount of goodwill.

Note:
- **Increase in the value of an Asset and decrease in the value of a liability result in profit.**

Assets A/c Dr.

To Revaluation
- **Decrease in the value of any asset and increase in the value of a liability gives loss.**

Revaluation A/c Dr.

To Assets A/c

- **For increase in the value of liabilities.**

Revaluation A/c Dr.

To Liabilities A/c

(Increase in value of Liability)

- **For decrease in the value of Liabilities**

Liabilities A/c Dr.

To Revaluation A/c
(Decrease in the value of Liabilities)

- **When Revaluation account shows profit**
Revaluation A/c Dr.
To Partner's Capital A/c
(Profit credited to Partner's Capital A/c in old ratio)

- **In case of Revaluation Loss**
Partner's Capital A/c's Dr.
To Revaluation A/c
(Loss debited to Partner's Capital A/c's in old ratio)

Accounting treatment for revaluation of assets and re-assessment of liabilities

The assets and liabilities are generally revalued at the time of admission of a new partner. Revaluation Account is prepared for this purpose in the same way was in case of change in profit sharing ratio. This account is debited with all losses and credited with all gains. Balance of Revaluation Account is transferred to old partner in their old ratio.

Accumulated profits and losses

Accumulated profits and reserves are distributed to partners in their old profit sharing ratio. If old partners are not interested to distribute, these accumulated profits are adjusted in the same manner as goodwill and the following adjusting entry will be passed.

New Partner's capital A/c Dr. (New share)
To old partner's capital A/c (Sacrificing ratio)

Revaluation Account

Revaluation account or profit and loss adjustment account are the same.

We need to bring the value of assets and liabilities to their current values otherwise the incoming partner may have an advantage because of the change in values.
- Credit the increase in the value of assets or decrease in the number of liabilities to revaluation account, being profit.
- Debit the decrease in value of assets or increase in the number of liabilities to revaluation account, being a loss.
- The difference between the two sides of the revaluation account is either profit or loss.

Particulars	Amount	Particulars	Amount
To Provision for doubtful debts	500	By Stock A/c	3,000
To Machinery A/c	2,000	By Land and Building A/c	14,700
To Furniture A/c	1,250	By Investments	2,000
To Outstanding electricity A/c	5,000	By Prepaid insurance A/c	5,000
To Profit transferred to:			
A 7,975			
B 7,975	15,950		
	24,700		24,700

If the credit side is more than debit side there is profit and if the debit side is more than the credit side there is a loss.
Transfer the Profit or loss of revaluation account to the partners capital accounts (old partners account) in their old profit sharing ratio.
There are two ways to revalue assets and liabilities:
1. Assets and Liabilities may appear in books at revised values.
2. Assets and Liabilities may appear at old values in books.

When assets and liabilities appear in the books at revised values.

Accounting entries are:

Date	Particulars		Amount (Dr.)	Amount (Cr.)
1. Increase in value of assets	Assets A/c	Dr.		
	To Revaluation A/c			
	(Being value of assets increased)			
2. A decrease in value of assets	Revaluation A/c	Dr.		
	To Assets A/c			
	(Being value of assets decreased)			
3. Increase in the number of liabilities	Revaluation A/c	Dr.		
	To Liabilities A/c			
	(Being increase in liabilities)			
4. A decrease in the amount of liabilities	Liabilities A/c	Dr.		
	To Revaluation A/c			
	(Being decrease in liabilities)			
5. Unrecorded assets	Unrecorded assets A/c	Dr.		
	To Revaluation A/c			
	(Being unrecorded asset now recorded)			
6. Unrecorded liabilities	Revaluation A/c	Dr.		
	To Unrecorded liabilities A/c			
	(Being unrecorded liability now recorded)			
7. Revaluation profit	Revaluation A/c	Dr.		
	To partners capital A/c			
	(Being profit transferred to partners capitals accounts)			
8. Revaluation loss	Partners capital A/c	Dr.		
	To revaluation A/c			
	(Being loss transferred to partners capital accounts)			

Revaluation Account

Particulars	Amount	Particulars	Amount
To Decrease in assets		By Increase in assets	
To Increase liabilities		By Decrease in liabilities	
To Unrecorded liabilities		By Unrecorded assets	
To Profit transferred to old partners capital accounts		By Loss transferred to old partners capital accounts	

When we prepare the Revaluation a/c, we show the assets and liabilities at their revised values in the balance sheet.

When assets and liabilities are to appear in the books at old values.

The partners may decide that the value of assets and liabilities will continue to appear in the books at their existing values. In such a case, we record an increase or decrease in the number of assets and liabilities in the Memorandum Revaluation Account. This account has two parts:

- The first part is much alike the revaluation account. Thus, we transfer the balance of the first part to old partners capital accounts in their old ratio.
- In the second part, we reverse the entries of the first part.

Thus, if the first part shows a profit than the second part will show loss and vice versa.

Admission of a partner

When a new partner is admitted in a running business due to the requirement of more capital or may be to take advantage of the experience and competence the newly admitted partner or any other reason, it is called admission of a part in partnership firm. According to section 31(1) of Indian partnership Act, 1932, "A new partner be admitted only with the consent of all the existing partners".

Profit sharing ratio

When old ratio is given and share of new partner is given.

Unless agreed otherwise, it is presumed that the new partner acquires his share in profits from the old partners in their old profit sharing ratio.

Alternative Method:

Old Ratio = A : B = 1 : 2

Left the profit of the firm = 1

C's share (New Partner) = 1/3

Remaining Profit = 1-1/3 = 2/3

Now this profit 2/3 will be divided between the old partners in their future profit sharing ratio (old ratio) i.c., 1:2

A's new Profit $= 1/3$ of $2/3 = \frac{1}{3} \times \frac{2}{3} = 2/9$

B's new Profit $= 2/3$ of $2/3 = \frac{2}{3} \times \frac{2}{3} = 4/9$

C's profit $= 1/3$ or $\frac{1}{3} \times \frac{3}{3} = 3/9$

Hence the new ratio = 2:4:3

Note: In this case only New Partners share is given then Sacrificing ratio = Old

Accounting Treatment of Goodwill

Goodwill, in accounting terms, is referred to as an intangible asset that represents the value created by the firm. The meaning of goodwill is very broad and is mostly used at times when one company acquires another company.

Goodwill is the price which companies are willing to pay for acquiring the other company at a price, which is in excess of its market value.

When computing for the partnership enterprises, the accounting treatment of goodwill in diverse scenarios is significant :

- The retiring or deceased partner is authorised to his portion of goodwill during the death or retirement because the goodwill has been earned by the enterprise with the hard work and perseverance of all the existing partners
- Hence, during the death/ retirement of a partner, goodwill is evaluated as per agreement among the partners the deceased/retiring partner recompensed for his portion of goodwill by the continuing partners (who have gained due to the accretion of the share of gain from the retiring/dead partner) in their respective gaining ratio.

In such a scenario, the accounting treatment for goodwill will rely on whether or not goodwill already exists in the company books.

Accounting treatment for revaluation of assets and re-assessment of liabilities

The assets and liabilities are generally revalued at the time of admission of a new partner. Revaluation Account is prepared for this purpose in the same way was in case of change in profit sharing ratio. This account is debited with all losses and credited with all gains. Balance of Revaluation Account is transferred to old partner in their old ratio.

Treatment of Reserves

The term reserves mean the profit amount, which is set aside with a purpose to utilise in need. In Accounting terms, this has been referred to as appropriation. Every reserve account carries a name which indicates its purpose or its use. Reserve account is a part of the net worth of the company. Thus, this can be said that reserve is an amount that is positioned on the liability side of the financial statement.

Accumulated profits and losses

Accumulated Profits and Losses is the sum of an enterprise's profits and losses left, after the dividend is paid. It can also be termed as either retained capital, retained earnings or earned surplus.

Sometimes, an enterprise might have accrued profits but not yet transferred to capital accounts of the partners. These are usually in the form of general reserve, reserve fund and/or Profit and Loss account balance. However, the new partner is not entitled to have any share in such accumulated profits. These are only allocated among the old partners by transferring it to their capital A/c in old profit sharing ratio. Correspondingly, if there are some accrued losses in the form of a Dr (Debit) balance of Profit and Loss account appearing in the balance sheet of the firm.

Adjustment of Capitals

An adjustment of capital is an adjustment that is made in an account in order to adjust for the effect of inflation because of the change in the prices of goods and/or services used by the business. Here, stocks are excluded but items such as prepaid expenses, receivable bills, and trade debtors are included.

Sometimes, at the time of admission, the partners agree that their capitals should also be adjusted so as to be proportionate to their profit sharing ratio. In such a situation, if the capital of the new partner is given, the same can be used as a base for calculating the new capitals of the old partners. The capitals thus ascertained should be compared with their old capitals after all adjustments relating to goodwill reserves and revaluation of assets and liabilities, etc. have been made; and then the partner whose capital falls short, will bring in the necessary amount to cover the shortage and the partner who has a surplus, will withdraw the excess amount of capital.

Current account and Balance sheet

A current account is a type of deposit account that caters to professionals and businessmen. Dealing largely with liquid deposits, this product allows for withdrawal of funds and checks being written against the balance and does not limit the number of transactions in a day.

A balance sheet is a financial statement that contains details of a company's assets or liabilities at a specific point in time. It is one of the three core financial statements (income statement and cash flow statement being the other two) used for evaluating the performance of a business.

Retirement and death of a partner

Like admission and changes in profit sharing ratio in case of retirement or death also the existing partnership deep comes to end and the new once comes into exist- tense among the remaining partner. There is not much difference in the accounting treatment at the time of retirement or in the event of death.

Effect of retirement

A partner may ascertain to either withdraw or retire from the enterprise due to certain reasons such as his bad health, his age, change in enterprise's nature of a business, etc., In the Partnership at Will, a partner might retire at any time. Retirement leads to a reconstitution of an enterprise where the partners' contribution ratio and the profit sharing ratio change. The retiring partner is given his share of capital, revaluation profit or loss and goodwill.

Preparation of loan account of the retiring partner

The remaining partners can pay the final amount payable to the retiring partner as a lump sum payment or may treat it as loan and repay in installments. The partners treat the amount due to the retiring partner as a loan from the partner so that they don't have to arrange the finance immediately from outside.

However, the retiring partner also enjoys the interest income in this case. Sometimes, the remaining partners repay the amount of loan in equal installments with interest on the balance amount. In such case, we divide the loan into equal parts and calculate the interest on the balance amount. The installment will consist of principal plus interest.

Calculation of deceased partner's share of profit till the date of death

In case of death of a partner during the year, his/her executer is entitled for share of profit up to the date of death of the partner. The share of profit can be calculated by one of the two methods.

1. **On time basis:** Under this method, profit up to the date of the death of the partner is calculated on the basis of the last year's/years' profit or average profit of last few years. In this approach, it is assumed that the profit will be uniform throughout the current year. The deceased partner will be entitled for the share of the profit proportionately up to the date of his/her death.
2. **On the sale basis:** Under this method, profit is calculated on the basis of last year's sale. In this situation, it is assumed that the net profit margin of the current year's sale is similar to that of the last year's.

Preparation of deceased partner's capital account and his executor's account

On the death of a partner, the partnership ceases to exist. But the firm may not cease to exist as the other remaining partners may decide to continue the business. In case of death of a partner, the treatment of various items is similar to that at the time of retirement of the partner. After making all the adjustments in the Partners Capital Account, the amount that is due to him is paid to his Legal Representative.

Adjustment of Partners Capital and Death of a Partner

At the time of the death of a partner, we credit the following amounts in the Deceased Partner's Capital Account

- Reserves or Undistributed profits.
- Goodwill.
- Profit on Revaluation of assets and liabilities.
- Any loan is given by the partner.
- The share of Joint Life Policy.
- Share in subsequent Profits.

- Interest on Capital.

Dissolution of Partnership

Dissolution of partnership and dissolution of the partnership firm are two different concepts. The dissolution of a partnership means a change of business relationship between partners whereas the dissolution of a firm means dissolving of the firm along with the relation between partners. In this case, all the assets and liabilities are settled and appropriately disposed.

Dissolution of partnership is said to take place when one of the partners associated with the business, ceases to be a part of the business going forward. It is very different from the termination of partnership. Dissolution can be defined as the process that ultimately leads to the termination of partnership. After dissolution, the remaining partners carry on the partnership but, this partnership is a completely new and different partnership.

Partnership firm

Dissolution of Partnership Firm identifies the distinction in the breaking of the association between all the partners of an enterprise and between a few partners; and it is the breaking or adjournment of the association between the partners which is known as the dissolution of partnership firm. This puts an end to the presence of an enterprise and no business concern is carried out after the dissolution apart from the pursuits associated with winding up of the enterprise as the financial affairs of the enterprise are to be affected by selling enterprise's assets.

When the current partnership is dissolved, the enterprise may go on under the same name if the partners determine. To put it in other words, it outcomes in the dissolution of a partnership however, not that of the enterprise. Section 39 of the partnership Act 1932 says, the dissolution of a partnership between all the partners of an enterprise is known as the dissolution of the firm.

Types of Dissolutions

While learning how is a firm dissolved, students must note these ways mentioned below:

1. **Dissolution by Agreement:** A firm can be dissolved with an agreement among its existing partners, though it should meet the following criteria:
- Every partner of a firm must consent to its dissolution.
- There must be legally binding contracts among existing partners.

2. **Mandatory Dissolution:** Circumstances under which a firm is dissolved compulsorily are as follows:
- When one or more partners of a firm become insolvent, making them incompetent to enter any contract or agreement.
- If it becomes unlawful for a specific partnership firm to continue its business and revenue generation. Notably, this is not the same as that of dissolution by court order. An example in this regard would be when a partnership firm has a foreign partner and war is declared by this firm's country of origin on that of its foreign partner. Under such circumstances, this firm must be dissolved.

3. **Emergency Dissolution Due to Contingencies:** A firm can be dissolved based on an existing contract among its partners only under these circumstances that are listed below:
- If a firm was established for a fixed tenure and that term has expired.
- If a firm was established for a specific venture and that venture has been completed.
- A partner's demise.
- If a partner of a firm becomes insolvent.

4. **Dissolution by Notice:** If the partnership of a firm is at will, one of its partners can issue a notice for its dissolution. It must be issued in writing to all the existing partners and clearly state his/her intention towards dissolving a firm.

5. **Dissolution by the Court:** When one of the partners of a firm files a legal suit, a court of law can direct the dissolution of a firm. That can be done on any of the following grounds described below.
- If a partner loses mental stability.
- If one partners becomes incapable of fulfilling his/her duties.
- When a partner is found guilty of any misconduct that goes on to affect this firm's business adversely.
- If one or more partners turn their whole interest in the partnership to a third party.
- When a lawful court deems its dissolution just.

Settlement of Accounts

Accounts settlement after the dissolution of a firm, are directed by provisions included in the Indian Partnership Act, 1932. These provisions mention these following guidelines.

1. A firm will pay for its losses and liabilities, including capital deficiency from its profits. If this profit is inadequate to clear its losses, a firm must pay for it from its partners' capital. If it still does not clear all a firm's losses, partners will have to clear it in the same ratio as that of their profit sharing.

2. When the firm is dissolved, its assets are applied to make for existing deficiencies and losses. The firm should begin by clearing third-party debts, followed by loans and advances made by any partner. Once these debts are cleared, the capital of every partner must be cleared. If a firm still has surplus funds, it should be divided among partners in the same ratio as that of profit-sharing.

Capital accounts of partners

The partnership capital account is an equity account in the accounting records of a partnership. It contains the following types of transactions:

- Initial and subsequent contributions by partners to the partnership, in the form of either cash or the market value of other types of assets.
- Profits and losses earned by the business, and allocated to the partners based on the provisions of the partnership agreement.
- Distributions to the partners.

Cash Account

A cash account is a type of brokerage account in which the investor must pay the full amount for securities purchased. An investor using a cash account is not allowed to borrow funds from his or her broker-dealer in order to pay for transactions in the account (trading on margin).

The credit extension provisions of the Federal Reserve Board's Regulation to govern an investor's use of a cash account to purchase securities. In a cash account, an investor must pay for the purchase of a security before selling it. If an investor buys and sells a security before paying for it, the investor is "freeriding" which is not permitted under Regulation T and may require the investor's broker to "freeze" the investor's cash account for 90 days. During this 90-day period, an investor may still purchase securities with the cash account, but the investor must fully pay for any purchase on the date of the trade.

Bank Account

A bank account is a place for you to deposit and withdraw funds, make payments, transfer money to another person or institution, pay bills electronically, and more. Bank accounts enable you to spend without cash on hand and get direct deposits from employers or other institutions.

Multiple Choice Questions

1. Features of a partnership firm are:
   - **A.** Two or more persons are carrying common business under an agreement.
   - **B.** They are sharing profits and losses in the fixed ratio.
   - **C.** Business is carried by all or any of them acting tor all as an agent.
   - **D.** All of the above.

Answer: D

Explanation:

In a partnership firm, two or more individuals come together to carry out a common business under an agreement. They share the profits and losses of the business in a predetermined ratio. Additionally, each partner has the authority to act on behalf of the partnership, making them agents for the firm.

2. Following are essential elements of a partnership firm except:
   - **A.** At least two persons
   - **B.** There is an agreement between all partners
   - **C.** Equal share of profits and losses
   - **D.** Partnership agreement is for some business.

Answer: C

Explanation:

The essential elements of a partnership firm include the presence of at least two persons, an agreement between all partners, and the partnership agreement being for some business. However, having an equal share of profits and losses is not a necessary element of a partnership firm. Partners may agree on different profit-sharing ratios based on their capital contributions or other factors.

3. In case of partnership the act of any partner is:
    A. Binding on all partners
    B. Binding on that partner only
    C. Binding on all partners except that particular partner
    D. None of the above

Answer: A

Explanation:

In a partnership, the act of any partner is binding on all partners. This means that the actions, agreements, or decisions made by any partner within the scope of the partnership's business will be legally binding on all other partners.

4. Which of the following statement is true?
    A. A minor cannot be admitted as a partner
    B. A minor can be admitted as a partner, only into the benefits of the partnership
    C. A minor can be admitted as a partner but his rights and liabilities are same of adult partner
    D. None of the above

Answer: B

Explanation:

A minor can be admitted as a partner, but only into the benefits of the partnership. This means that while a minor can receive a share of the profits, they do not have full rights and liabilities of an adult partner. The minor's involvement is limited to enjoying the benefits of the partnership without being held fully responsible for its obligations.

5. Oustensible partners are those who?
    A. do not contribute any capital but get some share of profit for lending their name to the business
    B. contribute very less capital but get equal profit
    C. do not contribute any capital and without having any interest in the business, lend their name to the business
    D. contribute maximum capital of the business

Answer: C

Explanation:

Oustensible partners are those who do not contribute any capital and do not have any interest in the business but lend their name to the business. They are essentially individuals who allow their names to be associated with the partnership, giving the appearance that they are partners, even though they have no actual financial or operational involvement in the business. Their role is primarily to provide credibility or attract customers.

6. Sleeping partners are those who?
    A. take active part in the conduct of the business but provide no capital. However, salary is paid to them.
    B. do not take any part in the conduct of the business but provide capital and share profits and losses in the agreed ratio
    C. take active part in the conduct of the business but provide no capital. However, share profits and losses in the agreed ratio.
    D. do not take any part in the conduct of the business and contribute no capital. However, share profits and losses in the agreed ratio.

Answer: B

Explanation:

Sleeping partners are those who do not take an active part in the conduct of the business but provide capital and share profits and losses in the agreed ratio. They contribute financial resources to the partnership but are not involved in the day-to-day operations or decision-making of the business. Despite their limited involvement, they still have a share in the profits and losses based on the agreed-upon ratio.

7. The relation of partner with the firm is that of:
    A. An Owner
    B. An Agent
    C. An Owner and an Agent
    D. Manager

Answer: C

Explanation:

The relation of a partner with the firm is that of both an owner and an agent. As an owner, a partner has a financial interest in the firm and shares in the profits and losses. As an agent, a partner can act on behalf of the firm and bind the firm to contractual obligations. Therefore, the partnership relationship encompasses both ownership and agency roles.

8. Number of partners in a partnership firm may be:

    A. Maximum Two   **B.** Maximum Ten

    C. Maximum One Hundred   **D.** Maximum Fifty

Answer: D

Explanation:

The number of partners in a partnership firm may be a maximum of fifty. The Partnership Act does not impose any restrictions on the minimum number of partners, but it sets a limit of fifty partners for ordinary partnerships. However, certain types of partnerships, such as banking or professional partnerships, may have different maximum limits as specified by their respective governing laws or regulations.

9. Liability of partner is:

    A. Limited   **B.** Unlimited

    C. Determined by Court   **D.** Determined by Partnership Act

Answer: B

Explanation:

The liability of a partner in a partnership is unlimited. This means that the partners are personally liable for the debts, obligations, and liabilities of the partnership. If the partnership assets are insufficient to cover the debts, the personal assets of the partners can be used to satisfy the liabilities. The partners have joint and several liability, meaning they can be held individually or collectively responsible for the partnership's obligations.

10. Which one of the following is NOT an essential feature of a partnership?

    A. There must be an agreement   **B.** There must be a business

    C. The business must be carried on for profits   **D.** The business must be carried on by all the partners

Answer: D

Explanation:

The business being carried on by all the partners is not an essential feature of a partnership. In a partnership, the business can be carried on by all the partners or by any of them acting on behalf of the partnership. It is not necessary for every partner to be actively involved in the day-to-day operations of the business. The other options, having an agreement, engaging in a business, and carrying on the business for profits, are essential features of a partnership.

11. Every partner is bound to attend diligently to his _____________ in the conduct of the business.

    A. Rights   **B.** Meetings

    C. Capital   **D.** Duties

Answer: D

Explanation:

Every partner is bound to attend diligently to his duties in the conduct of the business. Partners have a duty to engage in the management and operations of the partnership actively and responsibly. This includes fulfilling their responsibilities, making informed decisions, and carrying out their assigned tasks diligently for the benefit of the partnership.

12. Forming a Partnership Deed is:

    A. Mandatory   **B.** Mandatory in Writing

    C. Not Mandatory   **D.** None of the Above

Answer: C

Explanation:

Forming a Partnership Deed is not mandatory. While it is highly recommended and advisable to have a written Partnership Deed, it is not legally required to establish a partnership. Partnerships can be created through an oral agreement or even implied by the actions and conduct of the partners. However, having a written Partnership Deed helps clarify the rights, responsibilities, profit-sharing ratios, and other terms agreed upon by the partners, providing a clear framework for the partnership's operations.

13. Partnership Deed is also called:

    A. Prospectus   **B.** Articles of Association

    C. Principles of Partnership   **D.** Articles of Partnership

Answer: D

Explanation:

Partnership Deed is also called Articles of Partnership. It is a legal document that outlines the terms and conditions of a partnership. The Partnership Deed typically includes details such as the name of the partnership, the names of the partners, their capital contributions, profit-sharing ratios, decision-making processes, and other important provisions governing the partnership.

14. Which of the following is not incorporated in the Partnership Act?

    A. Profit and loss are to be shared equally   **B.** No interest is to be charged on capital

    C. All loans are to be charged interest @6% p.a.   **D.** All drawings are to be charged interest

Answer: D

Explanation:

The provision that all drawings are to be charged interest is not incorporated in the Partnership Act. The Partnership Act does not specify any requirement for charging interest on drawings made by partners. The Act primarily governs the formation, rights, and obligations of partners, profit sharing, capital contributions, and other key aspects of partnership, but it does not address the charging of interest on partner drawings.

15. Which one of the following is NOT an essential feature of a partnership?

    A. There must be an agreement   **B.** There must be a business

    C. The business must be carried on for profits   **D.** The business must be carried on by all the partners

Answer: D

Explanation:

The business being carried on by all the partners is not an essential feature of a partnership. While a partnership can be carried on by all the partners, it is not a requirement. The Partnership Act allows for the business to be carried on by any of the partners, as long as it is done within the scope of the partnership agreement. The other options, having an agreement, engaging in a business, and carrying on the business for profits, are essential features of a partnership.

16. If any loan or advance is provided by partner then, balance of such Loan Account should be transferred to:

    A. B/S Assets side   **B.** B/S Liability Side

    C. Partner's Capital A/C   **D.** Partner's Current A/C

Answer: B

Explanation:

If any loan or advance is provided by a partner, the balance of such Loan Account should be transferred to the Balance Sheet's Liability Side. This is because the loan provided by a partner represents an obligation or liability of the partnership towards that partner. It is important to reflect this liability on the Balance Sheet to accurately represent the financial position of the partnership.

17. Is rent paid to a partner appropriation of profits:

    A. It is appropriation of profit   **B.** It is not appropriation of profit

    C. If partner's contribution as capital is maximum   **D.** If partner is a working partner.

Answer: B

Explanation:

Rent paid to a partner is not an appropriation of profits. Rent is a business expense incurred for the use of property or assets owned by the partner. It is treated as an expense in the income statement and reduces the partnership's taxable income. It does not directly impact the distribution of profits among the partners.

18. What should be the minimum number of persons to form a Partnership:

    A. 2   **B.** 7

    C. 10   **D.** 20

Answer: A

Explanation:

The minimum number of persons required to form a partnership is 2. According to the Indian Partnership Act, 1932, a partnership can be formed by a minimum of two individuals who come together with the intention of carrying on a business and sharing its profits and losses.

19. In case of partnership the act of any partner is :

    A. Binding on all partners   **B.** Binding on that partner only

    C. Binding on all partners except that particular partner   **D.** None of the above

Answer: A

Explanation:

In a partnership, the act of any partner is binding on all partners. This means that the actions, agreements, or decisions made by any partner within the scope of the partnership's business will be legally binding on all other partners. Each partner has the authority to bind the partnership, and their actions have implications for all partners.

20. A and B are partners in a partnership firm without any agreement. A devotes more time for the firm as compare to B. A will get the following commission in addition to profit in the firm's profit:

    A. 6 % of profit   **B.** 4 % of profit

    C. 5 % of profit   **D.** None of the above

Answer: D

Explanation:

In the absence of any agreement, A would not be entitled to any additional commission on the firm's profits. Without a specific provision in the partnership agreement, the distribution of profits would typically be based on the agreed profit-sharing ratio among the partners. The scenario of A devoting more time than B does not automatically entitle A to an additional commission.

21. In the absence of agreement, partners are not entitled to:

    A. Salary   **B.** Commission

    C. Equal share in profit   **D.** Both (A) and (B)

Answer: D

Explanation:

In the absence of an agreement, partners are not entitled to receive a salary or commission. Without a specific provision in the partnership agreement, partners do not have the right to receive a fixed salary or commission for their services. Instead, their entitlement to a share in the profits would be determined based on the agreed profit-sharing ratio or as per the provisions of the Partnership Act.

22. In case of partnership the act of any partner is :

    A. Binding on all partners   **B.** Binding on that partner only

    C. Binding on all partners except that particular partner   **D.** None of the above

Answer: A

Explanation:

In a partnership, the act of any partner is binding on all partners. This means that the actions, agreements, or decisions made by any partner within the scope of the partnership's business will be legally binding on all other partners. Each partner has the authority to bind the partnership, and their actions have implications for all partners.

23. In the absence of partnership deed, partners share profits or losses:

    A. In the ratio of their Capitals   **B.** In the ratio decided by the court

    C. Equally   **D.** In the ratio of time devoted

Answer: C

Explanation:

In the absence of a partnership deed, partners share profits or losses equally. This means that each partner would receive an equal share of the profits and bear an equal share of the losses incurred by the partnership. This default rule is outlined in the Indian Partnership Act, 1932, in the absence of any agreement specifying a different profit-sharing ratio.

24. Features of a partnership firm are:

    A. Two or more persons are carrying common business under an agreement.   **B.** They are sharing profits and losses in the fixed ratio.

    C. Business is carried by all or any of them acting tor all as an agent.   **D.** All of the above.

Answer: D

Explanation:

To form a partnership, there must be an agreement between two or more persons to carry on a common business. The partners share the profits and losses in a predetermined ratio, and they can act as agents for the partnership, conducting business on behalf of all partners. Therefore, the correct option is D, as it encompasses all the mentioned features of a partnership.

25. The persons who have entered into partnership are individually known as :

    A. Partners   **B.** Firm

    C. Associations   **D.** None of these

Answer: A

Explanation:

The persons who have entered into a partnership are individually known as partners. A partnership is formed when two or more individuals come together to carry on a business and share its profits and losses. Each individual in the partnership is referred to as a partner and has rights, responsibilities, and liabilities within the partnership.

26. Which one of the following is NOT an essential feature of a partnership:
- **A.** There must be an agreement
- **B.** There must be a business
- **C.** The business must be carried on for profits
- **D.** The business must be carried on by all the partners

Answer: D

Explanation:

The business being carried on by all the partners is not an essential feature of a partnership. While a partnership can be carried on by all the partners, it is not a requirement. The Partnership Act allows for the business to be carried on by any of the partners, as long as it is done within the scope of the partnership agreement. The other options, having an agreement, engaging in a business, and carrying on the business for profits, are essential features of a partnership.

27. A partner introduced additional capital of ₹30,000 and advanced a loan of ₹40,000 to the firm at the beginning of the year. Partner will receive year's interest:
- **A.** ₹ 4,200
- **B.** ₹ 2,400
- **C.** Nil
- **D.** ₹ 1,800

Answer: B

Explanation:

To calculate the partner's interest on the loan advanced to the firm, we need to know the agreed interest rate. Assuming an interest rate of 6% per annum, the interest on the loan of ₹40,000 would be ₹2,400 for the year (₹40,000 × 6% = ₹2,400).

28. Which of the following items are recorded in the Profit & Loss Appropriation Account of a partnership firm:
- **A.** Interest on Capital
- **B.** Salary to Partner
- **C.** Transfer to Reserve
- **D.** All of the above

Answer: D

Explanation:

All of the above items, namely interest on capital, salary to partner, and transfer to reserve, are recorded in the Profit & Loss Appropriation Account of a partnership firm. The Profit & Loss Appropriation Account is used to allocate the profits among the partners based on the agreed profit-sharing ratio. Interest on capital represents the return on the partners' investments, salary to partner is the remuneration paid for their services, and transfers to reserve are provisions for retaining a portion of the profits for future use.

29. Interest on capital will be paid to the partners if provided for in the partnership deed but only out of:
- **A.** Profits
- **B.** Reserves
- **C.** Accumulated Profits
- **D.** Goodwill

Answer: A

Explanation:

Interest on capital will be paid to the partners only out of profits. If the partnership deed specifies that partners are entitled to receive interest on their capital contributions, such interest payments will be made from the profits generated by the partnership. It is important to note that interest on capital is not paid from reserves, accumulated profits, or goodwill.

30. Intangible Assets (Goodwill) has been defined in:
- **A.** AS 16
- **B.** AS 20
- **C.** AS 26
- **D.** AS 21

Answer: C

Explanation:

Goodwill, including intangible assets, is defined in Accounting Standard (AS) 26. AS 26 provides guidance on the measurement, recognition, and disclosure of intangible assets, including goodwill. It outlines the criteria for recognizing and measuring goodwill and provides guidelines on impairment testing and disclosure requirements for intangible assets.

Chapter-2   Accounting for Companies

Introduction

A company form of organization is the third stage in the evolution of forms of organization. Its capital is contributed by a large number of persons called shareholders who are the real owners of the company. But neither it is possible for all of them to participate in the management of the company nor considered desirable. Therefore, they elect a Board of Directors as their representative to manage the affairs of the company. In fact, all the affairs of the company are governed by the provisions of the Companies Act, 2013. A company means a company incorporated or registered under the Companies Act, 2013 or under any other earlier Companies Acts. According to Chief Justice Marshal, "a company is a person, artificial, invisible, intangible and existing only in the eyes of law. Being a mere creation of law, it possesses only those properties which the charter of its creation confers upon it, either expressly or as incidental to its very existence".

A company usually raises its capital in the form of shares (called share capital) and debentures (debt capital.) This chapter deals with the accounting for share capital of companies.

Features of a Company

A company may be viewed as an association of person who contribute money or money's worth to a common inventory and use it for a common purpose. It is an artificial person having corporate legal entity distinct from its members (shareholders) and has a common seal used for its signature. Thus, it has certain special features which distinguish it from the other forms of organisation. These are as follows:

- Body Corporate: A company is formed according to the provisions of Law enforced from time to time. Generally, in India, the companies are formed and registered under Companies Law except in the case of Banking and Insurance companies for which a separate Law is provided for.
- Separate Legal Entity: A company has a separate legal entity which is distinct and separate from its members. It can hold and deal with any type of property. It can enter into contracts and even open a bank account in its own name.
- Limited Liability: The liability of the members of the company is limited to the extent of unpaid amount of the shares held by them. In the case of the companies limited by guarantee, the liability of its members is limited to the extent of the guarantee given by them in the event of the company being wound up.
- Perpetual Succession: The company being an artificial person created by law continues to exist irrespective of the changes in its membership. A company can be terminated only through law. The death or insanity or insolvency of any member of the company in no way affects the existence of the company. Members may come and go but the company continues.
- Common Seal:The company being an artificial person, cannot sign its name by itself. Therefore, every company is required to have its own seal which acts as official signatures of the company. Any document which does not carry the common seal of the company is not binding on the company.
- Transferability of Shares: The shares of a public limited company are freely transferable. The permission of the company or the consent of any member of the company is not necessary for the transfer of shares. But the Articles of the company can prescribe the manner in which the transfer of shares will be made.
- May Sue or be Sued: A company being a legal person can enter into contracts and can enforce the contractual rights against others. It can sue and be sued in its name if there is a breach of contract by the company.

Kinds of Companies

Companies can be classified either on the basis of the liability of its members or on the basis of the number of members. On the basis of liability of its members the companies can be classified into the following three categories:

Companies Limited by Shares: In this case, the liability of its members is limited to the extent of the nominal value of shares held by them. If a member has paid the full amount of the shares, there is no liability on his part whatsoever may be for the debts of the company. He need not pay a single paise from his private property. However, if there is any liability involved, it can be enforced during the existence of the company as well as during the winding up.

Companies Limited by Guarantee: In this case, the liability of its members is limited to the amount they undertake to contribute in the event of the company being wound up. Thus, the liability of the members will arise only in the event of its winding up.

Unlimited Companies: When there is no limit on the liability of its members, the company is called an unlimited company. When the company's property is not sufficient to pay off its debts, the private property of its members can be used for the purpose. In other words, the creditors can claim their dues from its members. Such companies are not found in India even though permitted by the Companies Act.

On the basis of the number of members, companies can be divided into three categories as follows:

Public Company: A public company means a company which (a) is not a private company; (b) is a company which is not a subsidiary of a private company.

Private Company: A private company is one which by its articles of association:

(a) Restricts the right to transfer its shares;

(b) A private company must have at least 2 persons, except in case of one person company;

(c) Limits the number of its members to 200 (excluding its employees);

One Person Company (OPC): Sec. 2 (62) of the companies Act, 2013, defines OPC as a "company which has only one person as a member". Rule 3 of the Companies (Incorporation) Rules, 2014 provides that:

(a) Only a natural person being an Indian citizen and resident in India can form one person company,

(b) It cannot carry out non-banking financial investment activities.

(c) Its paid up share capital is not more than Rs. 50 Lakhs

(d) Its average annual turnover of three years does not exceed Rs. 2 Crores.

Share Capital of a Company

A company, being an artificial person, cannot generate its own capital which has necessarily to be collected from several persons. These persons are known as shareholders and the amount contributed by them is called share capital. Since the number of shareholders is very large, a separate capital account cannot be opened for each one of them. Hence, innumerable streams of capital contribution merge their identities in a common capital account called as 'Share Capital Account'.

Categories of Share Capital

From accounting point of view the share capital of the company can be classified as follows:

Authorized Capital: Authorized capital is the amount of share capital which a company is authorized to issue by its Memorandum of Association. The company cannot raise more than the amount of capital as specified in the Memorandum of Association. It is also called Nominal or Registered capital. The authorized capital can be increased or decreased as per the procedure laid down in the Companies Act. It should be noted that the company need not issue the entire authorized capital for public subscription at a time. Depending upon its requirement, it may issue share capital but in any case, it should not be more than the amount of authorized capital.

Issued Capital: It is that part of the authorized capital which is actually issued to the public for subscription including the shares allotted to vendors and the signatories to the company's memorandum. The authorized capital which is not offered for public subscription is known as 'unissued capital'. Unissued capital may be offered for public subscription at a later date.

Subscribed Capital: It is that part of the issued capital which has been actually subscribed by the public. When the shares offered for public subscription are subscribed fully by the public the issued capital and subscribed capital would be the same. It may be noted that ultimately, the subscribed capital may be equal to or less than issued capital. In case the number of shares subscribed is less than what is offered, the company allots only the number of shares for which subscription has been received. In case it is higher than what is offered, the allotment will be equal to the offer. In other words, the fact of over subscription is not reflected in the books.

Called up Capital: It is that part of the subscribed capital which has been called up on the shares, i.e., what the company has asked the shareholders to pay. The company may decide to call the entire amount or part of the face value of the shares, For example, if the face value (also called nominal value) of a share allotted is Rs. 10 and the company has called up only Rs. 7 per share, in that scenario, the called up capital is Rs. 7 per share. The remaining Rs. 3 may be collected from its shareholders as and when needed.

Paid up Capital: It is that portion of the called up capital which has been actually received from the shareholders. When the shareholders have paid all the called amount, the called up capital is the same to the paid up capital. If any of the shareholders has not paid amount on calls, such an amount may be called as 'calls in arrears'. Therefore, paid up capital is equal to the called-up capital minus call in arrears.

Uncalled Capital: That portion of the subscribed capital which has not yet been called up. As stated earlier, the company may collect this amount any time when it needs further funds. - Reserve Capital: A company may reserve a portion of its uncalled capital to be called only in the event of winding up of the company. Such uncalled amount is called 'Reserve Capital' of the company. It is available only for the creditors on winding up of the company.

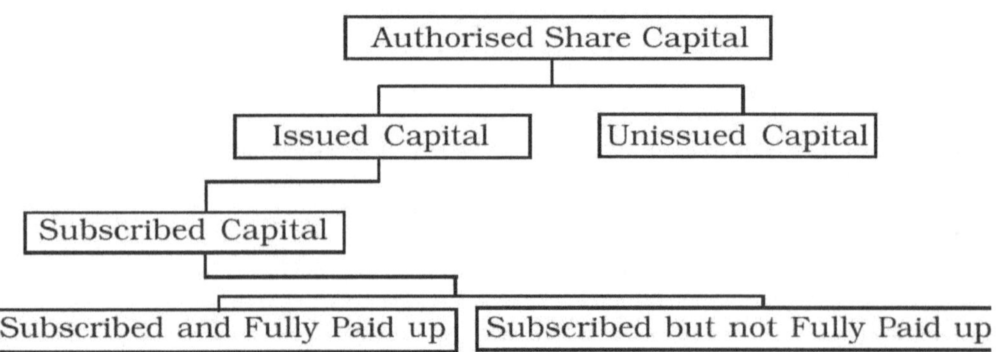

Let us take the following example and show how the share capital will be shown in the balance sheet. Sunrise Company Ltd., New Delhi, has registered its capital as Rs. 40,00,000, divided into 4,00,000 shares of Rs. 10 each. The company offered to the public for subscription of 2,00,000 shares of Rs. 10 each, to be received as Rs. 2 on application, Rs. 3 on allotment, Rs. 3 on first call and the balance on final call. The company received applications for 2,50,000 shares. The company finalised the allotment of 2,00,000 shares and rejected applications for 50,000 shares. The company did not make the final call. The company received all the amount except on 2,000 shares where call money has not been received.

The above amounts will be shown in the Notes to Accounts of the balance sheet of Sunrise Company Ltd. as follows:

Notes to Accounts

Share Capital		(Rs.)
Authorized or Registered or Nominal Capital:		
4,00,000 Shares of Rs. 10 each		
Issued Capital		
2,00,000 Shares of Rs. 10 each		
Subscribed Capital		
Subscribed but not fully paid up 2,00,000 Shares of Rs. 10 each, Rs. 8 called up Less : Calls in Arrears	16,00,000	

Nature and Classes of Shares

Shares, refer to the units into which the total share capital of a company is divided. Thus, a share is a fractional part of the share capital and forms the basis of ownership interest in a company. The persons who contribute money through shares are called shareholders.

The amount of authorized capital, together with the number of shares in which it is divided, is stated in the Memorandum of Association but the classes of shares in which the company's capital is to be divided, along with their respective rights and obligations, are prescribed by the Articles of Association of the company. As per The Companies Act, a company can issue two types of shares:

(1) Preference shares
(2) Equity shares (also called ordinary shares)

Preference Shares

According to Section 43 of The Companies Act, 2013, a preference share is one, which fulfils the following conditions :

(a) That it carries a preferential right to dividend to be paid either as a fixed amount payable to preference shareholders or an amount calculated by a fixed rate of the nominal value of each share before any dividend is paid to the equity shareholders.

(b) That with respect to capital it carries or will carry, on the winding up of the company, the preferential right to the repayment of capital before anything is paid to equity shareholders.

However, notwithstanding the above two conditions, a holder of the preference share may have a right to participate fully or to a limited extent in the surpluses of the company as specified in the Memorandum or Articles of the company. Thus, the preference shares can be participating and nonparticipating. Similarly, these shares can be cumulative or non-cumulative, and redeemable or irredeemable.

Equity Shares

According to Section 43 of The Companies Act, 2013, an equity share is a share which is not a preference share. In other words, shares which do not enjoy any preferential right in the payment of dividend or repayment of capital, are termed as equity/ordinary shares. The equity shareholders are entitled to share the distributable profits of the company after satisfying the dividend rights of the preference share holders. The dividend on equity shares is not fixed and it may vary from year to year depending upon the amount of profits available for distribution. The equity share capital may be (i) with voting rights; or (ii) with differential rights as to voting, dividend or otherwise in accordance with such rules and subject to such conditions as may be prescribed in the Articles of Association of the company.

Issue of Shares

A salient characteristic of the capital of a company is that the amount on its shares can be gradually collected in easy instalments spread over a period of time depending upon its growing financial requirement. The first instalment is collected along with application and is thus, known as application money, the second on allotment (termed as allotment money), and the remaining instalments are termed as first call, second call and so on. The word final is suffixed to the last instalment. However, this in no way which prevents a company from calling the full amount on shares right at the time of application.

The important steps in the procedure of share issue are :

- **Issue of Prospectus:** The company first issues the prospectus to the public. Prospectus is an invitation to the public that a new company has come into existence and it needs funds for doing business. It contains complete information about the company and the manner in which the money is to be collected from the prospective investors.
- **Receipt of Applications:** When prospectus is issued to the public, prospective investors intending to subscribe the share capital of the company would make an application along with the application money and deposit the same with a scheduled bank as specified in the prospectus. The company has to get minimum subscription within 120 days from the date of the issue of the prospectus. If the company fails to receive the same within the said period, the company cannot proceed for the allotment of shares and application money should be returned within 130 days of the date of issue of prospectus.
- **Allotment of Shares:** If minimum subscription has been received, the company may proceed for the allotment of shares after fulfilling certain other legal formalities. Letters of allotment are sent to those whom the shares have been alloted, and letters of regret to those to whom no allotment has been made. When allotment is made, it results in a valid contract between the company and the applicants who now became the shareholders of the company.

Shares of a company are issued either at par or at a premium. Shares are to be issued at par when their issue price is exactly equal to their nominal value according to the terms and conditions of issue. When the shares of a company are issued more than its nominal value (face value), the excess amount is called premium. Irrespective of the fact that shares are issued at par or at a premium, the share capital of a company as stated earlier, may be collected in instalments payable at different stages.

Accounting Treatment

On application: The amount of money paid with various instalment represents the contribution to share capital and should ultimately be credited to share capital. However, for the sake of convenience, initially individual accounts are opened for each instalment. All money received along with application is deposited with a scheduled bank in a separate account opened for the purpose.

The journal entry is as follows:
Bank A/c
Dr.
To Share Application A/c per share)
(Amount received on application for - shares @ Rs. On allotment: When minimum subscription has been received and certain legal
formalities on the allotment of shares have been duly compiled with, the directors of the company proceed to make the allotment of shares.
The allotment of shares implies a contract between the company and the applicants who now become the allottees and assume the status of shareholders or members.

 The journal entries with regard to allotment of shares are as follows:
1   For Transfer of Application Money
Share Application A/c Dr.
To Share Capital A/c
(Application money on __ Shares allotted/ transferred to Share Capital)
2   For Money Refunded on Rejected Application
Share Application A/c Dr.
To Bank A/c
(Application money returned on rejected application for
shares)

3   For Amount Due on Allotment
Share Allotment A/c Dr.
To Share Capital A/c
4   For Adjustment of Excess Application Money
Share Application A/c Dr.
To Share Allotment A/c
(Application Money on__Shares @ Rs__per shares
adjusted to the amount due on allotment).
5   For Receipt of Allotment Money
Bank A/c Dr.
To Share Allotment A/c
(Allotment money received on__Shares @
Rs. - per share Combined Account)

Note:- The journal entries (2) and (4) can also be combined as follows:
Share Application A/c
To Share Allotment A/c
To Bank A/c
(Excess application money adjusted to share
allotment and balance refunded)

Sometimes a combined account for share application and share allotment called 'Share Application and Allotment Account' is opened in the books of a company. The combined account is based on the reasoning that allotment without application is impossible while application without allotment is meaningless. These two stages of share capital are closely inter-related. When a combined account is maintained, journal entries are recorded in the following manner:
 1. For Receipt of Application and Allotment
Bank A/c Dr.
To Share Application and Allotment A/c
(Money received on applications for shares
@ Rs.__ per share).
2   For Transfer of Application Money and Allotment Amount Due
Share Application and Allotment A/c Dr.
To Share Capital A/c
(Transfer of application money to Share Capital Account for amount due or allotment of - Share @ Rs. per share)
3   For Money Refunded on Rejected Applications
Share Application and Allotment A/c Dr.
To Bank A/c
(Application money returned on rejected application for __ shares)
4   On Receipt of Allotment Amount
Bank A/c
Dr.
To Share Application and Allotment A/c
(Balance of Allotment Money Received)

On Calls : Calls play a vital role in making shares fully paid-up and for realising the full amount of shares from the shareholders. In the event of shares not being fully called up till the completion of allotment, the directors have the authority to ask for the remaining amount on shares as and when they decide about the same. It is also possible that the timing of the payment of calls by the shareholders is determined at the time of share issue itself and given in the prospectus.

Two points are important regarding the calls on shares. First, the amount on any call should not exceed 25% of the face value of shares. Second, there must be an interval of at least one month between the making of two calls unless otherwise provided by the articles of association of the company.

When a call is made and the amount of the same is received, the journal entries are as given below:
1   For Call Amount Due
Share Call A/c Dr.
To Share Capital A/c
(Call money due on __Shares @ Rs.
per share)

2   For Receipt of Call Amount
Bank A/c Dr.
To Share Call A/c
(Call money received)

The word/words First, Second, or Third must be added between the words "Share" and 'Call' in the Share Call account depending upon the identity of the call made. For example, in case of first call it will be termed as 'Share First Call Account', in case of second call it will be 'Share Second Call Account' and so on. Another point to be noted is that the words 'and Final' will also be added to the last call, say, if second call is the last call it will be termed as 'Second and Final Call' and if it is the third call which is the last call, it will be termed as 'Third and Final Call'. It is also possible that the whole balance after allotment may be collected in one call only. In that case the first call itself, shall be termed as the 'First and Final Call'.

Calls in Arrears

It may happen that shareholders do not pay the call amount on due date. When any shareholder fails to pay the amount due on allotment or on any of the calls, such amount is known as 'Calls in Arrears'/'Unpaid Calls'. Calls in Arrears represent the debit balance of all the calls account. Such amount shall appear as 'Note to Accounts (Refer Chapter 3). However, where a company maintains 'Calls in Arrears' Account, it needs to pass the following additional journal entry:
Calls in Arrears A/c
Dr.
To Share First Call Account A/c
To Share Second and Final Call Account A/c
(Calls in arrears brought into account)

The Articles of Association of a company may empower the directors to charge interest at a stipulated rate on calls in arrears. If the articles are silent in this regard, the rule contained in Table F shall be applicable which states that the interest at a rate not exceeding 10% p.a. shall have to be paid on all unpaid amounts on shares for the period intervening between the day fixed for payment and the time of actual payment thereof.

On receipt of the call amount together with interest, the amount of interest shall be credited to interest account while call money shall be credited to the respective call account or to calls in arrears account. When the shareholder makes the payment of calls in arrears together with interest, the entry will be as follows:

Bank A/c
Dr.
To Calls in Arrears A/c
To Interest on Calls in Arrears A/c
(Calls in arrears received with interest)
Note: If nothing is specified, there is no need to take the interest on calls in arrears account and record the above entry.

Illustration 3
Cronic Limited issued 10,000 equity shares of Rs. 10 each payable at Rs. 2.50 on application, Rs. 3 on allotment, Rs. 2 on first call, and the balance of Rs. 2.50 on second and final call. All the shares were fully subscribed and paid except of a shareholder having 100 shares who could not pay for second and final call. Give journal entries to record these transactions.

Solution:

Books of Cronic Limited Journal

Date	Particulars	L.F.	Debit Amount (Rs.)	Credit Amount (Rs.)
	Bank A/c Dr. To Equity Share Application A/c (Money received on applications for 10,000 shares @ Rs. 2.50 per share)		25,000	25,000
	Equity Share Application A/c Dr. To Equity Share Capital A/c (Transfer of application money on 10,000 shares to share capital)		25,000	25,000

	Equity Share Allotment A/c Dr. To Equity Share Capital A/c (Amount due on the allotment of 10,000 shares @ Rs. 3 per share)	30,000	30,000
	Bank A/c Dr. To Equity Share Allotment A/c (Allotment money received)	30,000	30,000
	Share First Call A/c Dr. To Equity Share Capital A/c (First call money due on 10,000 shares @ Rs. 2 per share)	20,000	20,000
	Bank A/c Dr. To Equity Share First Call A/c (First call money received)	20,000	20,000
	Share Second and Final Call A/c Dr. To Equity Share Capital A/c (Final call money due)	25,000	25,000
	Bank A/c Dr. Call in Arrears A/c Dr. To Equity Share Second and Final Call A/c (Final call money received except that of 100 shares)	24,750 250	25,000

Calls in Advance

Sometimes shareholders pay a part or the whole of the amount of the calls not yet made. The amount so received from the shareholders is known as "Calls in Advance". The amount received in advance is a liability of the company and should be credited to 'Call in Advance Account." The amount received will be adjusted towards the payment of calls as and when they becomes due. Table F of the Companies Act provides for the payment of interest on calls in advance at a rate not exceeding 12% per annum. The following journal entry is recorded for the amount of calls received in advance.

Bank A/c

Dr.

To Calls in Advance A/c

(Amount received on call in advance)

On the due date of the calls, the amount of 'Calls in Advance' is adjusted by the following entry :

Calls in Advance A/c

Dr.

To Particular Call A/c

(Calls in advance adjusted with the call money due)

The balance in 'Calls in Advance' account is shown as a separate item under the title Equity and Liabilities in the company's balance sheet under the head 'current liabilities', as sub-head 'others current liabilities'. It is not added to the amount of paid-up capital.

As 'Calls in Advance' is a liability of the company, it is under obligation, if provided by the Articles, to pay interest on such amount from the date of its receipt up to the date when appropriate call is due for payment. A stipulation is generally made in the Articles regarding the rate at which interest is payable. However, if Articles are silent on this account, Table F is applicable which provides for interest on calls in advance at a rate not exceeding 12% per annum.

The accounting treatment of interest on Calls in Advance is as follows:

1 For Payment of Interest

Interest on Calls in Advance A/c Dr.

To Bank A/c

(Interest paid on Calls in Advance)

OR

2 (a) For Interest due

Interest on Calls in Advance A/c Dr.

To Sundry Shareholder's A/c

(Interest paid on Calls in Advance)

2 (b) For InterestPaid

Sundry Shareholder's A/c Dr.

To Bank A/c

Illustration

Unique Pictures Limited was registered with an authorised capital of Rs. 5,00,000 divided into 20,000, 5% preference shares of Rs. 10 each and 30,000 equity shares of Rs. 10 each. The company issued 10,000 preference and 15,000 equity shares for public subscription. Calls on shares were made as under:

	Equity Shares Rs.	Preference Share Rs.
Application	2	2
Allotment	3	3
First Call	2.50	2.50
Second and Final Call	2.50	2.50

All these shares were fully subscribed. All the dues were received except the second and final call on 100 equity shares and on 200 preference shares. Record these transactions in the journal. You are also required to prepare the cash book and balance sheet.

Solution

Books of Unique Pictures Limited Journal

Date	Particulars		L.F.	Debit Amount (Rs.)	Credi Amoun (Rs.
	Equity Share Application A/c	Dr.		30,000	30,000
	5% Preference Share Application A/c	Dr.		20,000	20,000
	To Equity Share Capital A/c				
	To 5% Preference Share Capital A/c				
	(Transfer of application money)				
	Equity Share Allotment A/c	Dr.		45,000	45,000
	5% Preference Share Allotment A/c	Dr.		30,000	30,000
	To Equity Share Capital A/c				
	To 5% Preference Share Capital A/c				
	(Amount due on allotment)				
	Equity Share First Call A/c	Dr.		37,500	37,500
	5\% Preference Share First Call A/c	Dr.		25,000	25,000
	To Equity Share Capital A/c				
	To 5\% Preference Share Capital A/c				
	(First call money due)				
	Equity Share Second and Final Call A/c			37,500	37,500
	5\% Preference Share Second and final Call A/cDr.			25,000	25,000
	To Equity Share Capital A/c				
	To 5% Preference Share Capital A/c				
	(First call money due)				
	Call in Arrears A/c			750	250
	To Equity Share Second and Final Call A/c				500
	To 5\% Preference Share Final Call A/c				
	(For Calls in Arrears)				

Cash Book (Bank Column)

Date	Receipts	L.F.	Amount (Rs.)	Date	Payments	L.F.	Amount (Rs.)
	Equity Share Application A/c		30,000		Balance c/d		2,49,250
	5% Preference Share Application A/c		20,000				
	Equity Share		45,000				
	Allotment A/c 5% Preference		30,000				
	Share Allotment A/c Equity Share First Call A/c		37,500				
	5% Preference Share First Call A/c		25,000				
	Equity Share Second and Final Call A/c		37,250				
	5% Preference Share Second and Final Call A/c		24,500				
			2,49,250				2,49,250

Balance Sheet of unique pictures as at . . . .

Particulars	Note No.	Amount (Rs.)
I. Equity and Liabilities		
1. Shareholders' Funds		
a) Share capital	1	2,49,250
II. Assets		**2,49,250**
1. Current assets		
a) Cash and Cash Equivalents	2	2,49,250
		2,49,250

Over Subscription

There are instances when applications for more shares of a company are received than the number offered to the public for subscription. This usually happens in respect of shares issue of well-managed and financially strong companies and is said to be a case of 'Over Subscription'.

In such a condition, three alternatives are available to the directors to deal with the situation:
(1) they can accept some applications in full and totally reject the others;
(2) they can make a pro-rata allotment to all; and
(3) they can adopt a combination of the above two alternatives which happens to be the most common course adopted in practice. The problem of over subscription is resolved with the allotment of shares. Therefore, from the accounting point of view, it is better to place the situation of over subscription within the total frame of application and allotment, i.e. receipt of application amount, amount due on allotment and its receipt from the shareholders, and the same has been observed in the pattern of entries.

First Alternative: When the directors decide to fully accept some applications and totally reject the others, the application money received on rejected applications is fully refunded. For example, a company invited applications for 20,000 shares and received applications for 25,000 shares. The directors rejected the applications for 5,000 shares, which are in excess of the required number and refunded their application money in full.

In this case, the journal entries on application and allotment will be as follows:
The journal entries on application and allotment according to this alternative are as follows:
Bank A/c
Dr.
To Share Application A/c
(Money received on application for 25,000
shares @ Rs. _ per share)

Share Application A/c Dr.
To Share Capital A/c
To Bank A/c
(Transfer of application for money 20,000 for shares allotted and money refunded on
applications for 5,000 shares rejected)

Share Allotment A/c
Dr.
To Share Capital A/c
(Amount due on the allotment of 20,000 shares @ Rs. _ per share)

Bank A/c
Dr.
To Share Allotment A/c
(Allotment money received)

Second Alternative: When the directors opt to make a proportionate allotment to all applicants (called 'pro-rata' allotment), the excess application money received is normally adjusted towards the amount due on allotment. In case, the excess application money received is more than the amount due on allotment of shares, such excess amount may either be refunded or credited to calls in advance.

For example, in the event of applications for 20,000 shares being invited and those received are for 25,000 shares, it is decieded to allot shares in the ratio of 4:5 to all applicants. It is a case of pro-rata allotment and the excess application money received on 5,000 shares would be adjusted towards the amount due on the allotment of 20,000 shares.

In this case, the journal entries on application and allotment will be as follows.

1 Bank A/c Dr.
To Share Application A/c
(Application money received on 25,000 shares
@ Rs. _ per Share)
2 Share Application A/c Dr.
To Share Capital A/c
To Share Allotment A/c
(Transfer of application money to share
capital and the excess application money
on 5,000 shares credited to share allotment
account)
3
Share Allotment A/c
Dr.
To Share Capital A/c
(Amount due on allotment of 25,000 share
@ Rs. _ per share)
4
Bank A/c
Dr.
To Share Allotment A/c
(Allotment money received after adjusting
the amount already received as excess
application money)

Third Alternative: When the application for some shares are rejected outrightly; and pro-rata allotment is made to the remaining applicants, the money on rejected applications is refunded and the excess application money received from applicants to whom pro-rata allotment has been made is adjusted towards the amount due on the allotment of shares allotted.

For example, a company invited applications for 10,000 shares and received applications for 15,000 shares. The directors decided to reject the applications for 2,500 shares outright and to make a pro-rata allotment of 10,000 shares to the applicants for the remaining 12,500 shares so that four shares are allotted for every five shares applied. In this case, the money on applications for 2,500 shares rejected would be refunded fully and that on the remaining 2,500 shares (12,500 shares - 10,000 shares) would be adjusted against the allotment amount due on 10,000 shares allotted and credited to share allotment account, the journal entries on application and allotment recorded as follows:

1 Bank A/c
Dr.
To Share Application A/c
(Money received on application for 15,000
shares @ Rs. _ per share)
5
Share Application A/c
Dr.
To Share Capital A/c
To Share Allotment A/c
To Bank A/c
(Transfer of application money to share
capital, and the excess application amount of pro-rata allottees credited to share allotment and the amount on rejected applications refunded)
To Share Capital A/c
(Amount due on the Allotment of 10,000 shares @ Rs. _ per share)
To Share Allotment A/c
(Allotment money received after adjusting the amount already received as excess
application money)

Under Subscription

Under subscription is a situation where number of shares applied for is less than the number for which applications have been invited for subscription. For example, a company offered 2 lakh shares for subscription to the public but the applications were received for 1,90,000 shares, only. In such a situation, the allotment will be confirmed to 1,90,000 shares and entries shall be made accordingly. However, as stated earlier, it must be ensured that the company has received the minimum subscriptions and the company will have to refund the entire subscription amount received.

Issue of Shares at a Premium

It is quite common for the shares of financially strong and well-managed companies to be issued at a premium, i.e. at an amount more than the nominal or par value of shares. Thus, when a share of the nominal value of Rs. 100 is issued at Rs. 105 , it is said to have been issued at a premium of 5 per cent.

When the issue of shares is at a premium, the amount of premium may technically be called at any stage of the issue of shares. However, premium is generally called with the amount due on allotment, sometimes with the application money and rarely with the call money. The premium amount is credited to a separate account called 'Securities Premium Account' and is shown under the title 'Equity and Liabilities' of the company's balance sheet under the head 'Reserves and Surpluses'. It can be used only for the following five purposes:

(a) to issue fully paid bonus shares to the extent not exceeding unissued share capital of the company;

(b) to write-off preliminary expenses of the company;

(c) to write-off the expenses of, or commission paid, or discount allowed on any securities of the company; and

(d) to pay premium on the redemption of preference shares or debentures of the company.

(e) Purchase of its own shares (i.e., buy back of shares).

The journal entries for shares issued at a premium are as follows:

1   For Premium Amount called with Application money

(a) Bank A/c

Dr.

To Share Application A/c

(Money received on application for shares @ Rs. - per share including premium)

(b) Share Application A/c

Dr.

To Share Capital A/c

To Securities Premium Reserve A/c

(Transfer of application money to share

capital and securities premium account)

2   Premium Amount called with Allotment Money

(a) Share Allotment A/c Dr.

To Share Capital A/c

To Securities Premium Reserve A/c

(Amount due on allotment of shares @

Rs - per share including premium)

(b) Bank A/c

Dr.

To Share Allotment A/c

(Allotment money received including premium)

3   Premium Amount called with Call Money

(a) Share Application A/c

To Share Capital Reserve A/c

To Securities Premium A/c

(Amount due on $I^{st}/2^{nd}$ call @Rs − per share including premium)

(b) Bank A/c

Dr.

To Share Call A/c

(Call money received including premium)

Issue of Shares at a Discount

There are instances when the shares of a company are issued at a discount, i.e. at an amount less than the nominal or par value of shares, the difference between the nominal value and issue price representing discount on the issue of shares. For example, when a share of the nominal value of Rs. 100 is issued at Rs. 98, it is said to have been issued at a discount of two per cent.

As a general rule, a company cannot ordinarily issue shares at a discount. It can do so only in cases such as 'reissue of forfeited shares' (to be discussed later) and issue of sweat equity shares.

Issue of Shares for Consideration other than Cash

There are instances where a company enters into an arrangement with the vendors from whom it has purchased assets, whereby the latter agrees to accept, the payment in the form of fully paid shares of the company issued to them. Normally, no such cash is received for issue of shares. These shares can also be issued either at par, at premium or at discount, and the number of shares to be issued will depend upon the price at which the shares are issued and the amount payable to the vendor. The number of shares to be issued to the vendor will be calculated as follows:

Number of shares to be issued $= \dfrac{\text{Amount Payable}}{\text{Issue Price}}$

For example, Rahul Limited purchased building from Handa Limited for Rs.5,40,000 and the payment is to be made by the issue of shares of Rs. 100 each. The number of shares to be issued shall be worked out as follows in different situations:

(a) When shares are issued at par, i.e., at Rs. 100

Number of shares to be issued $= \dfrac{\text{Amount Payable}}{\text{Issue Price}}$

$= \dfrac{\text{Rs. 5,40,000}}{\text{Rs. 100}}$

= 5,400 shares

(b) When shares issued at premium of 20%, i.e., at Rs. 120(100 + 20)

Number of shares to be issued =

$= \dfrac{\text{Amount Payable}}{\text{Issue Price}}$

$= \dfrac{\text{Rs. 5,40,000}}{\text{Rs. 120}}$

= 4,500 Shares

The journal entries recorded for the shares issued for consideration other than cash in above situations will be as follows :

Books of Rahul Limited Journal

Date	Particulars	L.F	Debit Amount (Rs.)	Credit Amount (Rs.)
(a)	Building A/c To Handa Limited (Building purchased)		5,40,000	5,40,000
	When shares are issued at par Handa Limited To Share Capital A/c (5,400 Shares issued at par)		5,40,000	5,40,000
(b)	When shares are issued at premium of 20% Handa Limited To Share Capital A/c To Securities Premium Reserve A/c (4,500 shares issued at Rs. 120 per share)		5,40,000	5,40,000

Forfeiture of Shares

It may happen that some shareholders fail to pay one or more instalments, viz. allotment money and/or call money. In such circumstances, the company can forfeit their shares, i.e. cancel their allotment and treat the amount already received thereon as forfeited to the company within the framework of the provisions in its articles. These provisions are usually based on Table *F* which authorise the directors to forefeit the shares for non-payment of calls made. For this purpose, they have to strictly follow the procedure laid down in this regard. Following is the accounting treatment of shares issued at par, premium or at a discount. When shares are forfeited all entries relating to the shares forfeited except those relating to premium, already recorded in the accounting records must be reversed. Accordingly, share capital account is debited with the amount called-up in respect of shares are forfeited and crediting the respective unpaid calls accounts' or calls in arrears account with the amount already received. Thus, the journal entry will be as follows:

(a) Forfeiture of Shares issued at Par:

Share Capital A/c........(Called up amount)
Dr.

To Share Forfeiture A/c..........(Paid up amount)

To Share Allotment A/c

To Share Calls A/c (individually)

(..... shares forfeited for non-payment of

allotment money and calls made) It may be noted here that when the shares are forfeited, all entries relating to the forfeited shares must be reversed except the entry relating to share premium received, if any. Accordingly, the share capital is debited to the extent to called-up capital and credited to (i) respective unpaid calls account i.e., calls in arrears and (ii) share forfeiture account with the amount already received on shares.

The balance of shares forfeited account is shown as an addition to the total paid-up capital of the company under the head 'Share Capital' under title 'Equity and Liabilities' of the Balance Sheet till the forfeited shares are reissued.

Illustration

Honda Limited issued 10,000 equity shares of 100 each payable as follows: Rs. 20 on application, Rs. 30 on allotment, Rs. 20 on first call and Rs. 30 on second and final calls 10,000 shares were applied for and allotted. All money due was received with the exception of both calls on 300 shares held by Supriya. These shares were forfeited. Give necessary journal entries.

Solution

Books of Honda Limited Journal

Date	Particulars	L.F.	Debit Amount (Rs.)	Credit Amount (Rs.)
	Bank A/c To Equity Share Application A/c (Application money on 10,000 shares @Rs.20 per share received)		2,00,000	2,00,000
	Share Application A/c To Equity Share Capital A/c (Application money transferred to share capital)		2,00,000	2,00,000
	Share Allotment A/c To Equity Share Capital A/c (Money due on allotment of 10,000 shares @Rs. 30 per share)		3,00,000	3,00,000
	Bank A/c To Equity Share Allotment A/c (Allotment Money received on 10,000 shares @ Rs. 30 per share on)		3,00,000	3,00,000
	Share First Call A/c Dr To Equity Share Capital A/c (Money due on 10,000 shares @ Rs. 20 per share on Ist Call		2,00,000	2,00,000
	Bank A/c Dr To Equity Share First Call A/c (First call money received except for 300 shares)		1,94,000	1,94,000
	Share Second and Final Call A/c Dr. To Equity Share Capital A/c (Money due on 10,000 shares @ Rs. 30 per share on Second and Final Call)		3,00,000	3,00,000
	Bank A/c Dr To Equity Share Second and Final Call A/c (Second and Final Call money received except for 300 shares)		2,91,000	2,91,000

	Share Capital A/c Dr		30,000	
	To Equity Share First Call A/c			6,000
	To Equity Share Second and Final Call A/c			9,000
	To Share Forfeiture A/c			15,000
	(300 shares forfeited)			

Forfeiture of Shares issued at a Premium: If shares were initially issued at a premium and the premium amount has been fully realized, but some of the shares are forfeited due to non-payment of call money, the accounting treatment for forfeiture shall be on the same pattern as in the case of shares issued at par. The important point to be noted in this context is that the securities premium account is not to be debited at the time of forfeiture if the premium has been received in respect of the forefeited shares and the amount of forfeiture shall be excluding premium amount.

In case, however, if the premium amount has not been received, either wholly or partially, in respect of the shares forfeited, the Securities Premium Reserve Account will also be debited with the amount of premium not received along with the Share Capital Account at the time forfeiture. This will usually be the case when even the amount due on allotment has not been received. Thus, the journal entry to record the forfeiture of shares issued at a premium on which premium has not been fully received, will be :
Share Capital A/c Dr.
Securities Premium Reserve A/c
Dr.
To Share Forfeiture A/c To Share Allotment A/c
and/or
To Share Calls A/c (individually)
(..... shares forefeited for non-payment of
allotment money and calls made)
Note: If Calls in Arrears Account is maintained, Calls in Arrears Account is credited and not the Share Allotment and/or Share Call/Calls Accounts.

Reissue of Forfeited Shares

The directors can either cancel or re-issue the forfeited shares. In most cases, they reissue such shares which may be at par, at premium or at a discount. Forfeited shares may be reissued as fully paid at a par, premium, discount. In this context, it may be noted that the amount of discount allowed cannot exceed the amount that had been received on forfeited shares at the time of initial issue, and that the discount allowed on reissue of forfeited shares should be debited to the 'Forfeited Share Account'. The balance, if any, left in the Share-Forfeited Account relating to reissued Shares, should be treated as capital profit and transferred to Capital Reserve Account. For example, when a company forfeits 200 shares of Rs. 10 each on which Rs. 600 had been received, it can allow a maximum discount of Rs. 600 on their reissue. Assuming that the company reissues these shares for Rs. 1,800 as fully paid, the necessary journal entry will be:
Bank A/c
Share Forfeiture A/c
To Share Capital A/c Dr. 1,800
Dr. 200
2,000
(Reissue of 200 forfeited shares at Rs. 9 per
share as fully paid)
This shall leave a balance of Rs. 400 in share forfeited account which should be transferred to Capital Reserve Account by recording the following journal entry:
Share Forfeiture A/c
Dr. 400
To Capital Reserve 400
(Profit on reissue of forfeited shares
transferred) Another important point to be noted in this context is that the capital profit arises only in respect of the forfeited share reissued, and not on all forfeited shares. Hence, when a part of the forfeited shares are reissued, the whole balance of share forfeiture account cannot be transferred to the capital reserve. In such a situation, it is only the proportionate amount of balance that relates to the forfeited shares reissued which should be transferred to capital reserve, ensuring that the remaining balance in share forfeitures account is proportionate to the amount forfeited on shares not yet reissued.

Illustration
The director of Poly Plastic Limited resolved that 200 equity shares of Rs. 100 each be forfeited for non-payment of the second and final call of Rs.30 per share. Out of these, 150 shares were re-issued at Rs. 60 per share to Mohit.

Show the necessary journal entries .

Solution:

Books of Poly Plastic Limited Journal

Date	Particular	L.F.	Debit Amount (Rs.)	Credit Amount (Rs.)
	Share Capital A/c Dr.		20,000	
	To Shares Forfeiture A/c			14000
	To Share Second and Final Call A/c			6000
	(200 shares forfeited for non-payment of final call at Rs.30 per share)			
	Bank A/c Dr		9,000	
	Shares Forfeiture A/c Dr		6,000	
	To Share Capital A/c			15,000
	(Reissue of 150 shares of Rs.100 each, issued as fully paid for Rs.60 each)			
	Shares Forfeiture A/c Dr		4,500	
	To Capital Reserve A/c			4,500
	(Profit on reissue of 150 forfeited shares transferred to capital reserve)			

Working Notes :

Total amount forfeited on 200 shares

Amount forfeited on 150 shares

Amount of loss on reissue of 150 shares Rs.

$\quad$ = 14,000 (200 shares $\times$ Rs. 70)

$\quad$ = 10,500 (150 shares $\times$ Rs. 70)

$\quad$ = 6,000 (150 shares $\times$ Rs. 40)

Amount of profit on reissued shares

transferred to capital reserve $\quad$ = 4,500 (Rs. 10,500-Rs. 6,000)

Amount forfeited on 50 shares

= 3,500 (50 shares $\times$ Rs. 70)

Balance left in share forfeited account

= 3,500 (Rs. 14,000 $-$ Rs. 6,000

(equal to amount forfeited on 50 shares) Rs. 4,500)

Concept of Private Placement and Employee

A private placement is a sale of stock shares or bonds to pre-selected investors and institutions rather than publicly on the open market. It is an alternative to an initial public offering (IPO) for a company seeking to raise capital for expansion. Private placements are regulated by the U.S. Securities and Exchange Commission under Regulation D. Investors invited to participate in private placement programs include wealthy individual investors, banks and other financial institutions, mutual funds, insurance companies, and pension funds.

There are minimal regulatory requirements and standards for a private placement even though, like an IPO, it involves the sale of securities. The sale does not even have to be registered with the U.S. Securities and Exchange Commission (SEC). The company is not required to provide a prospectus to potential investors and detailed financial information may not be disclosed.

The sale of stock on the public exchanges is regulated by the Securities Act of 1933, which was enacted after the market crash of 1929 to ensure that investors receive sufficient disclosure when they purchase securities. Regulation D of that act provides a registration exemption for private placement offerings.

The same regulation allows an issuer to sell securities to a pre-selected group of investors that meet specified requirements. Instead of a prospectus, private placements are sold using a private placement memorandum (PPM) and cannot be broadly marketed to the general public.

Advantages and Disadvantages of Private Placement

Private placements have become a common way for startups to raise financing, particularly those in the internet and financial technology sectors. They allow these companies to grow and develop while avoiding the full glare of public scrutiny that accompanies an IPO.

As an example, Lightspeed Systems, an Austin-based company that creates content-control and monitoring software for K-12 educational institutions, raised an undisclosed amount of money in a private placement Series D financing round in March 2019. The funds were to be used for business development.

A Speedier Process
Above all, a young company can remain a private entity, avoiding the many regulations and annual disclosure requirements that follow an IPO. The light regulation of private placements allows the company to avoid the time and expense of registering with the SEC.

- That means the process of underwriting is faster, and the company gets its funding sooner.
- If the issuer is selling a bond, it also avoids the time and expense of obtaining a credit rating from a bond agency.
- A private placement allows the issuer to sell a more complex security to accredited investors who understand the potential risks and rewards.

A More Demanding Buyer
- The buyer of a private placement bond issue expects a higher rate of interest than can be earned on a publicly-traded security.
- Because of the additional risk of not obtaining a credit rating, a private placement buyer may not buy a bond unless it is secured by specific collateral.
- A private placement stock investor may also demand a higher percentage of ownership in the business or a fixed dividend payment per share of stock.

Types of Private Placements

Stock option
Pension funds and pension pools are frequently encouraged to participate in the non-public offering, allowing the issuing firm to raise a significant sum of money prior to the sale of any remaining shares of stock in an IPO. In this situation, individual investors can frequently acquire a sizeable stake in options that are expected to generate consistent returns over the long term.

Employee Stock Option is defined under Section 2(37) of the Companies Act, 2013. The employees stock option means the option provided to the directors, employees or officers of the company or its holding or subsidiary company, which gives the right or benefit to subscribe or purchase the shares of the company at a predetermined price on a future date. It is issued by a company when it wants to raise its subscribed capital. Rule 12 of Companies (Share Capital and Debentures) Rules, 2014 regulates the procedure of the issue of ESOP.

Sweat Equity Shares

Sweat Equity Share is defined under Section 2(88) of the Companies Act, 2013. The sweat equity shares mean shares issued by a company to its directors or employees for non-cash consideration or at a discount for making rights available in the nature of intellectual property rights or providing know-hows or any providing any value additions in any form. Rule 8 of Companies (Share Capital and Debentures) Rules, 2014 regulates the procedure of issue of sweat equity shares.

According to section 2(88), sweat equity shares mean such equity shares issued by a company to its directors or employees at a discount or for consideration, other than cash for providing their know-how or making available rights in the nature of intellectual property rights or value additions, by whatever name called.

According to Explanation to rule 8(1) of Companies (Share Capital and Debentures) Rules, 2014:For the purposes of this rule-The expressions "Employee" means:

- a permanent employee of the company who has been working in India or outside India;
- a director of the company, whether a whole-time director or not; or
- an employee or a director as defined in sub-clauses (a) or (b) above of a subsidiary, in India or outside India, or of a holding company of the company.

Section 54(1) provides that notwithstanding anything contained in Section 53, a company can issue sweat equity shares, of a class of shares already issued.

Forfeiture of shares can occur when some of the shareholders are unable to pay one or more of the installments, which can be allotment money or call money. In such situations, the company can forfeit the shares, which is cancelling their allotment.

After the shares are forfeited, the company can re-issue the shares, in this case it is known as re-issue of forfeited shares or reissue of shares.

For reissue of shares, the company can conduct an auction and dispose of the shares. The shares can be reissued at any price, but there is a clause, it states that the total money received on shares should not be less than the price of shares held in arrears.

The total amount includes the price paid by the first allottee and the price paid by the second purchaser.

This can be understood by the following example. Suppose, Arun paid Rs.4 for application money for a share having face value of Rs.10. He purchased 100 shares. Due to not being able to pay further installments, the company forfeits his shares and reissues them. Now, the amount that company has in arrear is Rs.6, so they can issue the shares at a value more than Rs.6 and not less than that.

The shares can be reissued at par, premium and discount. While there is no restriction on re-issue of shares at premium, there are certain restrictions on re-issue of shares at discount which are:
- For shares issued at par, the discount allowed is equal to value forfeited on these shares.
- For shares issued at discount, the original amount received first time becomes the forfeit amount. Maximum discount will be the sum of amount forfeited and amount of discount allowed at the time of first issue.
- For shares issued at premium, if premium is received the maximum discount will be the amount that is forfeited.

Conditions for Re-issue of Shares
There are four situations in which re-issue of shares take place.
- Forfeited shares reissued at discount when originally issued at par.
- Shares reissued at par or at premium, when originally issued at par.
- Forfeited shares reissued at par, at discount and at premium when originally issued at premium.
- Forfeited shares reissued at par, at discount and at premium, when originally issued at discount.

Let's look at the journal entries for the following cases

Forfeited shares reissued at discount when originally issued at par
When shares are reissued at a discount, the bank account will be debited by the amount received and the share capital account is credited by paid up amount. The discount allowed will be debited to share forfeited account.

Journal entries

Bank A/c (the amount received on reissue) Dr.
Share Forfeited A/c (the amount allowed as discount) Dr.
To Share Capital A/c (paid up amount)

If the amount of discount allowed is less than the forfeited amount then the remaining forfeited amount will be considered as a profit to the company and accordingly transferred to the capital reserve account

Share Forfeited A/c Dr.
To Capital Reserve A/c
(Transfer of surplus share forfeited amount to capital reserve A/c)

Shares reissued at par or at premium, when originally issued at par
In this case the whole amount that has been credited to Shares Forfeited A/c is transferred to capital reserve A/c

Journal entries

For shares reissued at par
Bank A/c Dr.

To Share Capital A/c

(Reissue of shares at ₹ per share)
Shares Forfeited A/c Dr.
To Capital Reserve A/c
(Balance amount of Shares Forfeited Account transferred to Capital reserve account)
For shares reissued at premium
Bank A/c Dr.
To Share Capital A/c
To Securities Premium Reserve A/c
(Reissue of forfeited shares at premium)
Share Forfeited A/c Dr.
To Capital Reserve A/c
(Balance amount of Shares Forfeited A/c is transferred to Capital Reserve A/c)

Forfeited shares reissued at par, at discount and at premium when originally issued at premium.
Shares that are originally issued at premium need not be reissued at premium, it can be reissued at par, discount or at premium
On reissuing at premium, the premium received should be credited to the Securities Premium A/c.

Journal entries

Bank A/c Dr.
(Number of shares × amount received per share)
To Share Capital A/c
(Number of shares × amount paid up per share)
To Securities Premium Reserve A/c
(Number of shares × amount of premium per share)

Forfeited shares reissued at par, at discount and at premium, when originally issued at discount.
When forfeited shares are originally issued at discount are reissued then discount allowed at the time of original issue is again applicable. On reissue of shares, the discount on issue of shares account is debited by the original discount amount.

Journal Entries

Share Capital A/c Dr.
To Share Forfeited A/c
To Discount on Issue of Shares A/c
To Share Final Call A/c
(Forfeiture of shares issued at discount)

Disclosure of share capital in the Balance Sheet of a company

A company has to raise funds to conduct its business. Since it is an artificial person, it cannot generate capital on its own. So it approaches investors for funds and issues shares (the total capital of a company gets divided into several units and each unit is called a share) as proof of their investment. These funds are collectively known as Share Capital.

Types of Share Capital

The different types of share capital are as follows:
Authorised Capital - It is the total amount of share capital that a company can issue to investors. It is also known as Normal or Registered Capital. This amount is present in the Memorandum of Association of that Company. They can increase or decrease the Authorised Capital after following the provisions mentioned in the Companies Act. The company doesn't have to issue shares for the entire amount at once. They can do it in tranches based on their need for funds.
Issued Capital - It is part of the Authorised Capital that the company has asked for investment from the general public for a subscription via shares. The leftover part is known as Unissued Capital. The company can issue that amount at a later date.
Subscribed Capital – Subscribed Capital is a part of the Issued Capital which the investors have taken via shares.
Called-up Capital – The portion of Subscribed Capital that the company has asked its shareholders to pay is the Called-up Capital. They can ask investors to pay the total amount or a part of the face value of shares.
Paid-up Capital – Paid-up Capital is the actual amount that the investors have paid to the company. If the shareholders haven't given a part of the called up amount, it is known as Calls in Arrears.

Uncalled Capital – It is the part of Subscribed Capital which the company hasn't asked its shareholders to pay yet. The company can ask for the amount when they require more funding.

Reserve Capital – Reserve Capital is that part of Uncalled Capital that the company may keep separate and use when it winds up its operations.

Disclosure of Share Capital in the Balance Sheet

Capital is present on the Liabilities side of the Balance Sheet of a company. The reason is that a company is an artificial person, and it owes the Capital amount to its owners and investors. Share Capital is present under the head Shareholders Fund.

We will explain how you can display the Share Capital in the Balance Sheet with the help of an example:

Question:

Zero Ltd. is a company that has an Authorised Share Capital amounting to Rs. 50 lakh divided into 50000 shares (the value of each share is Rs. 100). They offered 40000 shares to the general public under the following options:

Rs. 30 per share during application

Rs. 30 per share during allotment

Rs. 40 per share during the first call (it was also the final call)

The company got applications for 30000 shares. Out of those 30000 shares, they did not get the allotment money on 500 shares. They did not make the First Call for those shares. Kindly display the relevant items in the Balance Sheet of Zero Ltd.

Answer:

Balance Sheet of Zero Ltd.

As on ....

Equity and Liabilities	Note to	Current Year (₹)	Previous Year (₹)
Shareholder's Funds: 1. Share Capital*	(1)	17,85,000	
Assets			
Cash and Equivalents (Cash at Bank)		17,85,000	

*As per the revised Schedule VI, disclosure related to the Share Capital is provided in Notes to Accounts

Notes to Accounts

Equity and Liabilities		Current Year (₹)	Previous Year (₹)
(1) Share Capital:	18,00,000	50,00,000	
A. Authorised Capital	(15,000)	40,00,000	
50000 shares of Rs. 100 each		30,00,000	
B. Issued Capital		18,00,000	
40000 shares of Rs. 100 each		17,85,000	
C. Subscribed Capital			
30000 shares of Rs. 100 each			

D. Called-up Capital			
30000 shares of Rs. 100 each Rs 60 per share called up			
E. Paid-up Capital			
30000 shares of Rs. 100 each Rs 60 per share called up			
Less: Calls in Arrears (500 shares @Rs. 30 per share)			
Total		17,85,000	

Accounting for Debentures

A written instrument or document which is issued by the company acknowledging the borrowings is known as Debenture. In this document, the terms of repayment of principal and payment of interest at a specific rate are stated.

According to Section 2(30) of the Companies Act, 2013,"Debenture includes debenture stock, bonds and any other instrument of the company evidencing a debt, whether constituting a charge on the assets of the company or not."

According to Topham," A debenture is a document given by a company as evidence of a debt to the holder usually arising out of a loan and most commonly secured by a charge."

Characteristics of Debenture:
The characteristics of debentures are as follows:
- A debenture is a certificate or written document, which is an acknowledgement of debt taken by a company.
- It is borrowing of a company.
- It is issued under the seal of a company.
- Interests on Debentures is a charge against profit.
- It contains a contract for the repayment of the principal sum at a specified date.
- The funds raised by the issue of debentures are for a long period of time, such as 7 years, 10 years, or 12 years, and the loan raised by the issue of debentures is also called 'Loan Capital'.

Issue of Debentures:
A listed company can go for the issue of debentures for public subscription, but an unlisted company cannot issue debentures to the public in general. However, by private placement, both listed and unlisted companies may issue debentures. The accounting entries and procedures for issuing debentures are similar to that for the issue of shares. Debentures may be issued for cash; consideration other than cash; and as collateral security.
Debentures may be issued at par; premium; or at discount whether issued for cash or consideration other than cash.

Accounting Treatment of Issue of Debenture:
The journal entries passed for issuing debentures are the same as in the case of shares. Only 'Debenture A/c' is used in place of 'Share Capital A/c'. The rate of interest is usually pre-fixed with Debenture A/c.

On receipt of application money:

Date	Particulars		LF	Amount(Dr.)	Amount(Cr.)
	Bank A/c	Dr.		XXXX	
	To Debenture Application A/c				XXXX
	(Being application money received)				

On transfer of application money to Debenture A/c:

Date	Particulars		LF	Amount(Dr.)	Amount(Cr.)
	Debenture Application A/c	Dr.		XXXX	
	To x% Debenture A/c				XXXX
	(Being application money transferred to Debenture A/c)				

On allotment due:

Date	Particulars		LF	Amount(Dr.)	Amount(Cr.)
	Debenture Allotment A/c	Dr.		XXXX	
	To x% Debenture A/c				XXXX
	(Being debenture allotment)				

On receipt of allotment money:

Date	Particulars		LF	Amount(Dr.)	Amount(Cr.)
	Bank A/c	Dr.		XXXX	
	To Debenture Allotment A/c				XXXX
	(Being debenture allotment money received)				

On due of call money:

Date	Particulars		LF	Amount(Dr.)	Amount(Cr.)
	Debenture Call A/c	Dr.		XXXX	
	To x% Debenture A/c				XXXX
	(Being debenture allotment due)				

On receipt of call money:

Date	Particulars		LF	Amount(Dr.)	Amount(Cr.)
	Bank A/c	Dr.		XXXX	
	To Share First Call A/c				XXXX
	(Being first call money received on xxxx shares @ ₹XX per share)				

Presentation of Debenture A/c in Balance Sheet:

Balance Sheet of X Ltd.
as on D/M/Y

Particulars	Note No.	Amount (₹)
I. Equity and Liabilities		
(1) Shareholder's Fund:		
(a) Share Capital		XXXX
(b) Reserve & Surplus	1.	XXXX
(c) Money received against share warrants		XXXX
(2) Non-Current Liabilities:		
(a) Long-term borrowings	2.	XXXX
(b) Deferred tax liabilities (net)		XXXX
(c) Other Long term liabilities	3.	XXXX
(d) Long-term provisions		XXXX
Total		**XXXXX**
II. Assets		
(1) Non-Current Assets:		
(e) Other non-current Assets	4.	XXXX
(2) Current Assets:		
(f) Cash and Cash Equivalent	5.	XXXX
Total		**XXXXX**

Notes to Balance Sheet:

Note No.	Particulars	Amount (₹)
1	**Reserve and Surplus:**	
	Securities Premium Reserve	XXXX
2	**Long-term borrowings:**	
	8% Debentures	XXXX
3	**Other Long term liabilities:**	
	Premium on Redemption of Debentures	XXXX
4	**Other Current Assets:**	
	Discount on Issue of Debentures	XXXX
	Loss on Issue of Debentures	XXXX
5	**Cash and Cash Equivalents:**	
	Cash at Bank	XXXX

1. Which of the following is the element of financial statements?

    A. Balance Sheet   **B.** Profit & Loss A/c

    C. Both (A) and (B)   **D.** None of these

Answer: C

Explanation:

Balance Sheet, Profit & Loss A/c is the element of financial statements.

2. Which of the following is not required to be prepared under the Companies Act:

    A. Statement of Profit & Loss   **B.** Balance Sheet

    C. Auditor's Report   **D.** Fund Flow Statement

Answer: C

Explanation:

Auditor's Report is not required to be prepared under the Companies Act.

3. The reserve which is created for a particular (specific) purpose and which is a charge against revenue is called:

    A. Capital Reserve   **B.** General Reserve

    C. Secret Reserve   **D.** Specific Reserve

Answer: D

Explanation:

The reserve which is created for a particular (specific) purpose and which is a charge against revenue is called Specific Reserve.

4. An Annual Report is issued by a company to its:

    A. Directors   **B.** Authors

    C. Shareholders   **D.** Management

Answer: C

Explanation:

An Annual Report is issued by a company to its Shareholders.

5. The profit and loss disclosed by the accounts of a company is:

    A. Transferred to share capital account   **B.** Shown under the head of 'Current liabilities' and provisions

    C. Shown under the head 'Reserves and Surplus   **D.** None of these

Answer: C

Explanation:

The profit and loss disclosed by the accounts of a company is Shown under the head 'Reserves and Surplus.

6. The assets of a business can be classified as:

    A. Fixed and Non-fixed Assets   **B.** Tangible and Intangible Assets

    C. Non-Current and Current Asset   **D.** None of these

Answer: C

Explanation:

The assets of a business can be classified as Non-Current and Current Asset.

7. The term financial statements includes :

    A. Statement of Profit & Loss   **B.** Balance Sheet

    C. Statement of Profit & Loss and Balance Sheet   **D.** None of these

Answer: C

Explanation:

The term financial statements include Statement of Profit & Loss and Balance Sheet.

8. Balance Sheet is a:

    A. Account   **B.** Statement

    C. Both (A) and (B)   **D.** All the above

Answer: B

Explanation:

A balance sheet is a financial statement that contains details of a company's assets or liabilities at a specific point in time.

9. Financial statements are the product of accounting process:

- **A.** First
- **B.** Second
- **C.** End
- **D.** None of these

Answer: C

Explanation:

Financial statements are the product of accounting process is End.

10. Financial statements disclose:

- **A.** Monetary information
- **B.** Qualitative information
- **C.** Non-monetary information
- **D.** All the above

Answer: A

Explanation:

Financial statements disclose Monetary information.

11. Preliminary expenses are shown in the Balance Sheet under the head:

- **A.** Non-current assets
- **B.** Current assets
- **C.** Non-current liabilities
- **D.** Deducted from securities premium reserve

Answer: D

Explanation:

Preliminary expenses are shown in the Balance Sheet under the head Deducted from securities premium reserve.

12. Debit Balance of Profit & Loss Statement will be shown on:

- **A.** Assets Side of Balance Sheet
- **B.** Liabilities Side of Balance Sheet
- **C.** Under the head Reserve & Surplus
- **D.** Under the head Reserves and Surplus as a negative item

Answer: D

Explanation:

Debit Balance of Profit & Loss Statement will be shown on under the head Reserves and Surplus as a negative item.

13. Patents and copyrights fall under the category of:

- **A.** Current Assets
- **B.** Liquid Assets
- **C.** Intangible Assets
- **D.** None of these

Answer: C

Explanation:

Patents and copyrights fall under the category of Intangible Assets.

14. Goodwill falls under which category of assets:

- **A.** Current Assets
- **B.** Tangible Assets
- **C.** Intangible Assets
- **D.** None of the above

Answer: C

Explanation:

Goodwill falls under which category of assets intangible Assets.

15. Contingent Liabilities are exhibited under the heading:

- **A.** Fixed Liabilities
- **B.** Current Liabilities
- **C.** As a footnote
- **D.** None of these

Answer: C

Explanation:

Contingent Liabilities are exhibited under the heading as a footnote.

16. Provision for Provident Funds is shown in the Balance Sheet of a company under the head :

- **A.** Reserves and Surplus
- **B.** Non-current Liabilities
- **C.** Provision
- **D.** Contingent Liabilities

Answer: B

Explanation:

Provision for Provident Funds is shown in the Balance Sheet of a company under the head Non-current Liabilities.

17. Preliminary Expenses are shown in the Balance Sheet under which head?

    A. Fixed Assets   **B.** Reserves and Surplus

    C. Loans & Advances   **D.** None of these

Answer: D

Explanation:

Preliminary expenses are shown on the balance sheet under the head Misc. expenditure.

18. Financial Statements are:

    A. Anticipated facts   **B.** Recorded facts

    C. Estimated facts   **D.** None of these

Answer: B

Explanation:

Financial statements are prepared based on facts in the form of cost data recorded in accounting books. The original cost or historical cost is the basis of recording transactions.

19. The term current assets includes:

    A. Stock   **B.** Debtors

    C. Cash   **D.** All of these

Answer: D

Explanation:

Current assets include cash, cash equivalents, accounts receivable, stock inventory, marketable securities, pre-paid liabilities, and other liquid assets. Current Assets may also be called Current Accounts.

20. Which of the following is not a part of financial statement of a company ?

    A. Profit & Loss A/c   **B.** Balance Sheet

    C. Ledger Account   **D.** Cash Flow Statement

Answer: C

Explanation:

The Ledger Account is not a part of the financial statement of a company. The accounting ledger is used to generate the key financial statements the income statement, cash flow statement, and balance sheet for the company. "Posting" to an accounting ledger is the bookkeeping process of recording credits and debits.

21. Under which heading of Balance Sheet is general reserve shown:

    A. Miscellaneous Expenditure   **B.** Share Capital

    C. Reserves & Surplus   **D.** None of these

Answer: C

Explanation:

General reserves are shown on the liabilities side of the balance sheet under the head of reserves & surplus.

22. Current Assets on the Assets side of Balance Sheet of a Company includes:

    A. Sundry Debtors   **B.** Cash in hand

    C. Stock   **D.** All of these

Answer: D

Explanation:

Current assets include cash, cash equivalents, accounts receivable, stock inventory, marketable securities, pre-paid liabilities, and other liquid assets. The Current Assets account is important because it demonstrates a company's short-term liquidity and ability to pay its short-term obligations.

23. According to which part of Schedule III of the Indian Companies Act, 2013, Indian companies have to prepare Balance Sheet:

    A. Part 1   **B.** Part 2

    C. Part 3   **D.** Part 4

Answer: A

Explanation:

According to Part 1 of Schedule III of the Indian Companies Act, 2013, Indian companies have to prepare Balance Sheet.

24. Balance sheet of companies is now prepared in :

    A. Horizontal Form   **B.** Vertical Form

    C. Either (A) or (B)   **D.** None of these

Answer: B

Explanation:

The balance sheet of companies is now prepared in Vertical Form. A vertical balance sheet is one in which the accounting report format or design is shown in a sole column of numbers, starting with resource or asset details, trailed by liability details, and finishing with investors' value or shareholders' equity details.

25. The goodwill of a company is shown on the assets side of the Balance Sheet under the head.

    A. Current Assets   **B.** Non-current Assets

    C. Miscellaneous Expenditure   **D.** None of these

Answer: B

Explanation

The goodwill of a company is shown on the assets side of the Balance Sheet under the head Non-current Assets. Goodwill is recorded as an intangible asset on the acquiring company's balance sheet under the long-term assets account. Goodwill is considered an intangible (or non-current) asset because it is not a physical asset like buildings or equipment.

26. The form of Balance Sheet as per Companies Act, 2013 is:

    A. Horizontal   **B.** Horizontal or Vertical

    C. Vertical   **D.** None of these

Answer: C

Explanation:

The form of Balance Sheet as per Companies Act, 2013 is Vertical. All companies must maintain a vertical balance sheet as per section 129 of the Companies Act 2013. A vertical balance sheet is several columns beginning with liabilities and capital followed by all the assets.

27. Which of the following assets is not shown under the head 'Fixed Asset' in the Balance Sheet ?

    A. Goodwill   **B.** Bills Receivable

    C. Buildings   **D.** Vehicle

Answer: B

Explanation:

Bills Receivable is not shown under the head 'Fixed Asset' in the Balance Sheet. Bills receivable is a Current asset as it is repayable within 12 months. A bills receivable is a negotiable instrument/bill received from a customer in return of the goods purchased on credit. They are payable by the drawee on maturity.

28. Securities premium account is shown on the liabilities side in the balance sheet under heading:

    A. Reserves and Surplus   **B.** Current Liabilities and Provisions

    C. Share Capital   **D.** Contingent Liabilities

Answer: A

Explanation:

Securities premium account is shown on the liabilities side in the balance sheet under heading reserves and surplus.

29. Debentures are shown in the balance sheet under the head of:

    A. Short-term Loan   **B.** Secured Loan

    C. Current Liability   **D.** Share Capital

Answer: B

Explanation:

Debentures are shown in the balance sheet under the head of secured loan. Debentures are shown in the balance sheet of the company under the item Secured loans. Debentures are usually secured against the assets of the company. In case of debentures they are not secured by providing collateral or security.

30. Dividend is usually paid:

    A. On Authorized Capital   **B.** On Issued Capital

    C. On Paid-up Capital   **D.** On Called-up Capital

Answer: C

Explanation:

Dividend is usually paid in Paid-up Capital. Paid up Capital is the capital money received by the company against the shares sold. Hence, the dividends are paid only to those shareholders who have paid the money.

Introduction

You have learnt about the financial statements (Income Statement and Balance Sheet) of companies. Basically, these are summarized financial reports which provide the operating results and financial position of companies, and the detailed information contained therein is useful for assessing the operational efficiency and financial soundness of a company. This requires proper analysis and interpretation of such information for which a number of techniques (tools) have been developed by financial experts. In this chapter we will have an overview of these techniques.

Meaning of analysis of financial statements

The process of critical evaluation of the financial information contained in the financial statements in order to understand and make decisions regarding the operations of the firm is called 'Financial Statement Analysis'. It is basically a study of relationship among various financial facts and figures as given in a set of financial statements, and the interpretation thereof to gain an insight into the profitability and operational efficiency of the firm to assess its financial health and future prospects.

- It is a systematic process of dividing the financial information into simple and valuable elements, establishing relationships between inter-related elements and interpreting the same to understand the working and financial position of an enterprise from its financial statements.
- It includes analysis of Statement of Profit and Loss, Balance Sheet and Cash Flow Statement of an enterprise.
- It provides information to understand complex financial data and helps in taking appropriate financial decisions.

Understanding Analysis and Interpretation

These two terms in understanding the meaning of financial statement analysis are complementary to each other and therefore, analysis cannot be complete without interpretation.

Analysis: It is concerned with simplification of financial data by proper classification of given in the financial statement.

Interpretation: It is concerned with explaining the meaning and significance of the financial data.

Definition of Financial Statement Analysis:

As per Myer: Financial Statement Analysis is largely a study of relationships among the various financial factors in a business, as disclosed by a single set of statements, and a study of trends of these factors, as shown in a series of statements.

Significance of Analysis of Financial Statements

Financial analysis is the process of identifying the financial strengths and weaknesses of the firm by properly establishing relationships between the various items of the balance sheet and the statement of profit and loss. Financial analysis can be undertaken by management of the firm, or by parties outside the firm, viz., owners, trade creditors, lenders, investors, labour unions, analysts and others. The nature of analysis will differ depending on the purpose of the analyst. A technique frequently used by an analyst need not necessarily serve the purpose of other analysts because of the difference in the interests of the analysts. Financial analysis is useful and significant to different users in the following ways:

Finance manager

Financial analysis focusses on the facts and relationships related to managerial performance, corporate efficiency, financial strengths and weaknesses and creditworthiness of the company. A finance manager must be well-equipped with the different tools of analysis to make rational decisions for the firm. The tools for analysis help in studying accounting data so as to determine the continuity of the operating policies, investment value of the business, credit ratings and testing the efficiency of operations. The techniques are equally important in the area of financial control, enabling the finance manager to make constant reviews of the actual financial operations of the firm to analyse the causes of major deviations, which may help in corrective action wherever indicated.

Top management

The importance of financial analysis is not limited to the finance manager alone. It has a broad scope which includes top management in general and other functional managers. Management of the firm would be interested in every aspect of the financial analysis. It is their overall responsibility to see that the resources of the firm are used most efficiently and that the firm's financial condition is sound. Financial analysis helps the management in measuring the success of the company's operations, appraising the individual's performance and evaluating the system of internal control.

Trade payables

Trade payables, through an analysis of financial statements, appraises not only the ability of the company to meet its short-term obligations, but also judges the probability of its continued ability to meet all its financial obligations in future. Trade payables are particularly interested in the firm's ability to meet their claims over a very short period of time. Their analysis will, therefore, evaluate the firm's liquidity position.

Lenders

Suppliers of long-term debt are concerned with the firm's longterm solvency and survival. They analyse the firm's profitability over a period of time, its ability to generate cash, to be able to pay interest and repay the principal and the relationship between various sources of funds (capital structure relationships). Long-term lenders analyse the historical financial statements to assess its future solvency and profitability.

Investors

Investors, who have invested their money in the firm's shares, are interested about the firm's earnings. As such, they concentrate on the analysis of the firm's present and future profitability. They are also interested in the firm's capital structure to ascertain its influences on firm's earning and risk. They also evaluate the efficiency of the management and determine whether a change is needed or not. However, in some large companies, the shareholders' interest is limited to decide whether to buy, sell or hold the shares.

Labour unions

Labour unions analyse the financial statements to assess whether it can presently afford a wage increase and whether it can absorb a wage increase through increased productivity or by raising the prices.

Objectives of Analysis of Financial Statements

Analysis of financial statements reveals important facts concerning managerial performance and the efficiency of the firm. Broadly speaking, the objectives of the analysis are to apprehend the information contained in financial statements with a view to know the weaknesses and strengths of the firm and to make a forecast about the future prospects of the firm thereby, enabling the analysts to take decisions regarding the operation of, and further investment in the firm. To be more specific, the analysis is undertaken to serve the following purposes (objectives):

- To assess the current profitability and operational efficiency of the firm as a whole as well as its different departments so as to judge the financial health of the firm.
- To ascertain the relative importance of different components of the financial position of the firm.
- To identify the reasons for change in the profitability/financial position of the firm.
- To judge the ability of the firm to repay its debt and assessing the short-term as well as the long-term liquidity position of the firm.

Tools of Analysis of Financial Statements

Comparative Statements

These are the statements showing the profitability and financial position of a firm for different periods of time in a comparative form to give an idea about the position of two or more periods. It usually applies to the two important financial statements, namely, balance sheet and statement of profit and loss prepared in a comparative form. The financial data will be comparative only when same accounting principles are used in preparing these statements. If this is not the case, the deviation in the use of accounting principles should be mentioned as a footnote. Comparative figures indicate the trend and direction of financial position and operating results. This analysis is also known as 'horizontal analysis'.

As stated earlier, these statements refer to the statement of profit and loss and the balance sheet prepared by providing columns for the figures for both the current year as well as for the previous year and for the changes during the year, both in absolute and relative terms. As a result, it is possible to find out not only the balances of accounts as on different dates and summaries of different operational activities of different periods, but also the extent of their increase or decrease between these dates. The figures in the comparative statements can be used for identifying the direction of changes and also the trends in different indicators of performance of an organization.

The following steps may be followed to prepare the comparative statements:
Step 1 : List out absolute figures in rupees relating to two points of time (as shown in columns 2 and 3).
Step 2 : Find out change in absolute figures by subtracting the first year (Col.2) from the second year (Col.3) and indicate the change as increase (+) or decrease (−) and put it in column 4.

Step 3 : Preferably, also calculate the percentage change as follows and put it in column 5.

$$\frac{\text{Absolute Increase or Decrease (Col.4)}}{\text{First year absolute figure (Col.2}} \times 100$$

Particulars	First Year	Second Year	Absolute Increase (+) or Decrease (−)	Percentage Increase (+) or Decrease (−)
1	2	3	4	5
	Rs.	Rs.	Rs.	%.

Illustration

Convert the following statement of profit and loss of BCR Co. Ltd. into the comparative statement of profit and loss of BCR Co. Ltd.:

Particulars	Note No.	2015 − 16 (Rs.)	2016 − 17 (Rs.)
(i) Revenue from operations		60,00,000	75,00,000
(ii) Other incomes		1,50,000	1,20,000
(iii) Expenses		44,00,000	50,60,000
(iv) Income tax		35%	40%

Solution:

Comparative statement of profit and loss of BCR Co. Ltd. for the year ended March 31, 2016 and 2017:

Particulars	2015 − 16	2016 − 17	Absolute Increase (+ or Decrease (−)	Percentage Increase (+) or Decrease (−)
Revenue from operations	60,00,000	75,00,000	15,00,000	25.00
Add: Other incomes	1,50,000	1,20,000	30,000	20.00
Total Revenue I + II	61,50,000	76,20,000	14,70,000	23.90
Less: Expenses	44,00,000	50,60,000	6,60,000	15.00
Profit before tax	17,50,000	25,60,000	8,10,000	46.29
Less: Tax	6,12,500	10,24,000	4,11,500	67.18
Profit after tax	11,37,500	15,36,000	3,98,500	35.03

Illustration

From the following statement of profit and loss of Madhu Co. Ltd., prepare comparative statement of profit and loss for the year ended March 31, 2016 and 2017:

Particulars	Note No.	2015 − 16 (Rs.)	2016 − 17 (Rs.)
Revenue from operations		16,00,000	20,00,000
Employee benefit expenses		8,00,000	10,00,000
Other expenses		2,00,000	1,00,000
Tax rate 40%			

Solution:

Comparative statement of profit and loss of Madhu Co. Limited for the year ended March 31, 2016 and 2017:

Particulars	2015 − 16	2016-17	Absolute Increase (+ or or Decrease (-)	Percentage Increase (+) or Decrease (-)
	(Rs.)	(Rs.)	(Rs.)	%
I. Revenue from operations	**16,00,000**	**20,00,000**	**4,00,000**	**25**
II. Less- Expenses				
a) Employee benefit expenses	8,00,000	10,00,000	2,00,000	25
b) Other expenses	2,00,000	1,00,000	(1,00,000)	(50)

Profit before tax	6,00,000	9,00,000	3,00,000	50
III. Less tax @ 40%	2,40,000	3,60,000	1,20,000	50
Profit after tax	3, 60, 000	5,40,000	1,80,000	50

Common Size Statements

These are the statements which indicate the relationship of different items of a financial statement with a common item by expressing each item as a percentage of that common item. The percentage thus calculated can be easily compared with the results of corresponding percentages of the previous year or of some other firms, as the numbers are brought to common base. Such statements also allow an analyst to compare the operating and financing characteristics of two companies of different sizes in the same industry. Thus, common size statements are useful, both, in intra-firm comparisons over different years and also in making inter-firm comparisons for the same year or for several years. This analysis is also known as 'Vertical analysis'. 3. Trend Analysis: It is a technique of studying the operational results and financial position over a series of years. Using the previous years' data of a business enterprise, trend analysis can be done to observe the percentage changes over time in the selected data. The trend percentage is the percentage relationship, in which each item of different years bear to the same item in the base year. Trend analysis is important because, with its long run view, it may point to basic changes in the nature of the business. By looking at a trend in a particular ratio, one may find whether the ratio is falling, rising or remaining relatively constant. From this observation, a problem is detected or the sign of good or poor management is detected.

Common Size Statement, also known as component percentage statement, is a financial tool for studying the key changes and trends in the financial position and operational result of a company. Here, each item in the statement is stated as a percentage of the aggregate, or revenue from operations of which that item is a part. For example, a common size balance sheet shows the percentage of each asset to the total assets, and that of each liability to the total liabilities. Similarly, in the common size statement of profit and loss, the items of expenditure are shown as a percentage of the revenue from operations. If such a statement is prepared for successive periods, it shows the changes of the respective percentages over a period of time.

Common size analysis is of immense use for comparing enterprises which differ substantially in size as it provides an insight into the structure of financial statements. Inter-firm comparison or comparison of the company's position with the related industry as a whole is possible with the help of common size statement analysis.

The following procedure may be adopted for preparing the common size statements.
1   List out absolute figures in rupees at two points of time, say year 1, and year 2 (Column 2 & 4).
2   Choose a common base (as 100). For example, revenue from operations may be taken as base (100) in case of statement of profit and loss and total assets or total liabilities (100) in case of balance sheet.
3   For all items of Col. 2 and 3 work out the percentage of that total. Column 4 and 5 shows these percentages.

Particulars	Year one	Year two	Percentage of year 1	Percentage of year 2
1	2	3	4	5

Illustration

From the following information, prepare a Common size Income Statement for the year ended March 31, 2016 and March 31, 2017:

Particulars	2016 − 17 (Rs.)	2015 − 16 (Rs.)
Revenue from operations	18,00,000	25,00,000
Cost of good sold	10,00,000	12,00,000
Operating expenses	80,000	1,20,000
Non-operating expenses	12,000	15,000
Depreciation	20,000	40,000
Wages	10,000	20,000

Solution:

Common Size Income Statement
for the year ended March 31, 2016 and March 31, 2017

Particulars	Absolute Amounts		Percentage of Net Sales	
	2015 − 16 Rs.	2016 − 17 Rs.	2015-16 (%)	2016 − 17(%)
Revenue from operations	25,00,000	18,00,000	100	100
(Less) Cost of goods Sold*	12,00,000	10,00,000	48	55.56

Gross Profit	**13,00,000**	**8,00,000**	**52**	**44.44**
(Less) Operating Expenses**	1,20,000	80,000	4.80	4.44
Operating Income	**11,80,000**	**7,20,000**	**47.20**	**40**
(Less) Non-Operating expenses	15,000	12,000	0.60	0.67
Profit	**11,65,000**	**7,08,000**	**46.60**	**39.33**

* Wages is the part of cost of goods sold

** Depreciation is the part of operating expenses.

Ratio Analysis

It describes the significant relationship which exists between various items of a balance sheet and a statement of profit and loss of a firm. As a technique of financial analysis, accounting ratios measure the comparative significance of the individual items of the income and position statements. It is possible to assess the profitability, solvency and efficiency of an enterprise through the technique of ratio analysis.

Cash Flow Analysis

It refers to the analysis of actual movement of cash into and out of an organisation. The flow of cash into the business is called as cash inflow or positive cash flow and the flow of cash out of the firm is called as cash outflow or a negative cash flow. The difference between the inflow and outflow of cash is the net cash flow. Cash flow statement is prepared to project the manner in which the cash has been received and has been utilised during an accounting year as it shows the sources of cash receipts and also the purposes for which payments are made. Thus, it summarises the causes for the changes in cash position of a business enterprise between dates of two balance sheets.

Accounting Ratios

Ratio It is an arithmetical expression of relationship between two related or interdependent items. Accounting Ratios It is a mathematical expression that shows the relationship between various items or groups of items shown in financial statements. When ratios are calculated on the basis of accounting information, they are called accounting ratios. Ratio Analysis It is a technique which involves re-grouping of data by application of arithmetical relationship.

Objectives of Ratio Analysis

(i) To know the areas of an enterprise which need more attention.
(ii) To know about the potential areas which can be improved on.
(iii) Helpful in comparative analysis of the performance.
(iv) Helpful in budgeting and forecasting.
(v) To provide analysis of the liquidity, solvency, activity and profitability of an enterprise.
(vi) To provide information useful for making estimates and preparing the plans for future.

Advantages of Ratio Analysis

(i) It is useful in analysis of financial statements.
(ii) Helps in simplifying accounting figures.
(iii) Useful in judging the operating efficiency of business.
(iv) Helps in identification of problem areas.
(v) Helpful in comparative analysis.

Limitations of Ratio Analysis

(i) Accounting ratios ignore qualitative factors.
(ii) Absence of universally accepted terminology.
(iii) Ratios are affected by window-dressing.
(iv) Effects of inherent limitations of accounting.
(v) Misleading results in the absence of absolute data.
(vi) Price level changes ignored.
(vii) Affected by personal bias and ability of the analyst.

Classification of Accounting Ratios

Accounting or financial ratios can be broadly classified into two groups:

- Performance-related ratios
- Position-related ratios

Performance-related ratios

Performance-related ratios can be further classified into three groups: trading ratios, profitability ratios, and dividend ratios.

Trading ratios
These ratios relate to the trading aspect of the business. They are intended to help the management assess the effectiveness of the company's pricing policy, stock carrying, and speed of stock turnover.

The main trading ratios are:
- Gross profit ratio
- Rate of stock turnover
- Total assets turnover ratio
- Operating assets turnover ratio

Profitability ratios
As the name implies, these ratios help management in assessing the company's overall profitability. The important profitability ratios are:
- Return on equity ratio
- Return on capital employed ratio
- Net profit ratio
- Gross profit ratio
- Earnings per share ratio
- Price-earnings ratio
- Earnings yield rate

Dividend ratios
Dividend ratios disclose the company's dividend policy (i.e., to what extent does it distribute or retain its profits?). The ratios include:
- Dividend declared as a percentage of after-tax profit
- Dividend cover for preference shares
- Dividend cover for ordinary shares
- Dividend yield ratio

Position-related ratios
Position-related ratios fall into two sub-groups: capital-related ratios and liquidity-related ratios.

Capital-related ratios
These ratios relate to the company's capital structure. They show the relationship of each class of capital employed to the total capital employed. The important capital ratios are:
- Equity as a percentage of capital employed
- Borrowed capital as a percentage of capital employed
- Capital gearing ratio
- Gearing level
- Interest coverage ratio
- Fixed assets as a percentage of capital employed
- Working capital as a percentage of capital employed

Liquidity-related ratios
These ratios reflect the company's ability to meet its current liabilities out of current assets. The most commonly used liquidity ratios are:
- Current ratio
- Quick ratio or acid test ratio
- Debtors turnover ratio
- Average collection period
- Average payment period
- Average stock retention period
- Working capital cycle

Liquidity Ratios

Liquidity means the firm's ability to meet its current liabilities. In other words, the ability of a business to pay its short-term debts is frequently referred to as the liquidity position of the business. Short-term creditors of the firm are generally interested to know about the liquidity position of the firm. The liquidity ratio is further categorized into two parts: (i) Current Ratio & (ii) Liquid Ratio

Liquidity ratios determine how quickly a company can convert the assets and use them for meeting the dues that arise. The higher the ratio, the easier is the ability to clear the debts and avoid defaulting on payments.

This is a very important criterion that creditors check before offering short term loans to the business. An organisation which is unable to clear dues results in creating impact on the creditworthiness and also affects credit rating of the company.

Types of Liquidity Ratio

Current Ratio or Working Capital Ratio
The current ratio is a measure of a company's ability to pay off the obligations within the next twelve months. This ratio is used by creditors to evaluate whether a company can be offered short term debts. It also provides information about the company's operating cycle. It is also popularly known as Working capital ratio. It is obtained by dividing the current assets with current liabilities.

Current ratio is calculated as follows:
Current ratio = Current Assets / Current Liabilities
A higher current ratio around two (2) is suggested to be ideal for most of the industries while a lower value (less than 1) is indicative of a firm having difficulty in meeting its current liabilities.

Quick Ratio or Acid Test Ratio
Quick ratio is also known as Acid test ratio is used to determine whether a company or a business has enough liquid assets which are able to be instantly converted into cash to meet short term dues. It is calculated by dividing the liquid current assets by the current liabilities:

It is represented as
Quick Ratio = (Cash + Marketable securities + Accounts receivable) / Current liabilities
The ideal quick ratio should be one (1) for a financially stable company.

Solvency Ratios

A solvency ratio is a key metric used to measure an enterprise's ability to meet its long-term debt obligations and is used often by prospective business lenders. A solvency ratio indicates whether a company's cash flow is sufficient to meet its long-term liabilities and thus is a measure of its financial health.

Types of Solvency Ratios

Debt-Equity Ratio: Debt-Equity Ratio measures the relationship between long-term debt and equity. If debt component of the total long-term funds employed is small, outsiders feel more secure.

Debt-Equity Ratio = Long term Debts / Shareholders' Funds

Where:
Shareholders' Funds (Equity) = Share capital + Reserves and Surplus + Money received against share warrants
Share Capital = Equity share capital + Preference share capital
Or
Shareholders' Funds (Equity) = Non-current assets + Working capital – Non-current liabilities Working Capital = Current Assets – Current Liabilities

Example:
From the following information calculate Debt equity Ratio:-

Share capital: 10,000 shares of 10 each1,00,000 debentures   75,000

| General Reserve | 45000 Long term provision | 25,000 |
| Surplus | 30,000 Outstanding Expenses | 10,000 |

Solution:

Debt to equity ratio = Debt / Equity (shareholder funds) = 1,00,000 / 1,75,000 = 0.57 : 1

Debt = Debentures + Long term provisions = 75,000 + 25,000 = 1,00,000

Equity = Share Capital + General Reserve + Surplus = 1,00,000 + 45,000 + 30,000 = 1,75,000

Total Assets to Debt Ratio: This ratio measures the extent of the coverage of long-term debts by assets

Total assets to Debt Ratio = Total assets/Long-term debts

Example:

Shareholders' funds Rs. 1,40,000

Total Debts (Liabilities) Rs. 18,00,000

Current Liabilities = Rs. 2,00,000.

Calculate total assets to debt ratio.

Solution:

Total Assets to debt ratio = Total Assets / Long term Debts

= 32,00,000 / 16,00,000 = 2 : 1

Long term debts = total debts (Liabilities) – Current Liabilities

= 18,00,000 – 2,00,000 = 16,00,000

Total assets = shareholder funds + total debts (liabilities)

Proprietary Ratio: Proprietary ratio expresses relationship of proprietor's (shareholders) funds to net assets and is calculated as follows:

Proprietary Ratio = Shareholders, Funds / Capital employed (or net assets)

Significance: Higher proportion of shareholders' funds in financing the assets is a positive feature as it provides security to creditors. This ratio can also be computed in relation to total assets instead of net assets (capital employed)

Interest Coverage Ratio: It is a ratio which deals with the servicing of interest on loan. It is a measure of security of interest payable on long-term debts. It expresses the relationship between profits available for payment of interest and the amount of interest payable.

It is calculated as follows:

Interest Coverage Ratio = Net Profit before Interest and Tax / Interest on long-term debts

Significance: It reveals the number of times interest on long-term debts is covered by the profits available for interest. A higher ratio ensures safety of interest on debts.

Example:

From the following details, calculate interest coverage ratio:

Net Profit after tax Rs. 60,000; 15% Long-term debt 10,00,000; and Tax rate 40%.

Solution:

Net Profit after Tax = Rs. 60,000

Tax Rate = 40%

Net Profit before tax = Net profit after tax × 100/ (100 – Tax rate)

= Rs. 60,000 × 100/(100 – 40)

= Rs. 1,00,000

Interest on Long-term Debt = 15% of Rs. 10,00,000 = Rs. 1,50,000

Net profit before interest and tax = Net profit before tax + Interest

= Rs. 1,00,000 + Rs. 1,50,000 = Rs. 2,50,000

Interest Coverage Ratio = Net Profit before Interest and Tax/Interest on long-term debt

= Rs. 2,50,000/Rs. 1,50,000

= 1.67 times

These ratios indicate the speed at which, activities of the business are being performed. The activity ratios express the number of times assets employed. Higher turnover ratio means better utilisation of assets and signifies improved efficiency and profitability, and as such is known as efficiency ratios.

Inventory Turnover Ratio: It determines the number of times inventory is converted into revenue from operations during the accounting period under consideration. It expresses the relationship between the cost of revenue from operations and average inventory.

The formula for its calculation is as follows:
Inventory Turnover Ratio = Cost of Revenue from Operations / Average Inventory

Example:
From the following information, calculate inventory turnover ratio:
Inventory in the beginning = 18,000
Inventory at the end = 22,000
Net purchases = 46,000
Wages = 14,000
Revenue from operations = 80,000
Carriage inwards = 4,000

Solution:
Inventory Turnover Ratio = Cost of Revenue from Operations / Average Inventory
Cost of Revenue from Operations = Inventory in the beginning + Net Purchases + Wages + Carriage inwards − Inventory at the end
= Rs. 18,000 + Rs. 46,000 + Rs. 14,000 + Rs. 4,000 − Rs. 22,000 = Rs. 60,000
Average Inventory = Inventory in the beginning + Inventory at the end / 2
= Rs. 18,000 + Rs. 22,000/ 2 = Rs. 20,000
∴ Inventory Turnover Ratio = Rs. 60,000/ Rs. 20,000 = 3 Times

Trade Receivables Turnover Ratio: It expresses the relationship between credit revenue from operations and trade receivable. It is calculated as follows:
Trade Receivable Turnover ratio = Net Credit Revenue from Operations / Average Trade Receivable
Where Average Trade Receivable = (Opening Debtors and Bills Receivable + Closing Debtors and Bills Receivable)/2

Example:
Calculate the Trade receivables turnover ratio from the following information:
Total Revenue from operations 4,00,000
Cash Revenue from operations 20% of Total Revenue from operations
Trade receivables as at 1.4.2014 40,000
Trade receivables as at 31.3.2015 1,20,000

Solution:
Trade Receivables Turnover Ratio = Net Credit Revenue from Operations / Average Trade Receivables
Credit Revenue from operations = Total revenue from operations − Cash revenue from operations
Cash Revenue from operations = 20% of Rs. 4,00,000
= Rs. 4,00,000 × 20 / 100 = Rs. 80,000
Credit Revenue from operations = Rs. 4,00,000 − Rs. 80,000 = Rs. 3,20,000
Average Trade Receivables = Opening Trade Receivables + Closing Trade Receivables / 2
= Rs. 40,000 + Rs. 1,20,000 / 2 = Rs. 80,000
= Net Credit Revenue Form Operations / Average Inventory
= Rs. 3,20,000 / Rs. 80,000 = 4 times.

Trade Payable Turnover Ratio: Trade payables turnover ratio indicates the pattern of payment of trade payable. As trade payable arise on account of credit purchases, it expresses relationship between credit purchases and trade payable.
It is calculated as follows:

Trade Payables Turnover ratio = Net Credit purchases / Average trade payable
Where,
Average Trade Payable = (Opening Creditors and Bills Payable + Closing Creditors and Bills Payable)/2
Average Payment Period = No. of days/month in a year ÷Trade Payables Turnover Ratio

Example:
Calculate the Trade payables turnover ratio from the following figures:
Credit purchases during 2014-15 = 12,00,000
Creditors on 1.4.2014 = 3,00,000
Bills Payables on 1.4.2014 = 1,00,000
Creditors on 31.3.2015 = 1,30,000
Bills Payables on 31.3.2015 = 70,000

Solution:
Trade Payables Turnover Ratio = Net Credit Purchases / Average Trade Payables
Average Trade Payables = Creditors in the beginning + Bills payables in the beginning + Creditors at the end + Bills payables at the end / 2
= Rs. 3,00,000 + Rs. 1,00,000 + Rs. 1,30,000 + Rs. 70,000 2 = Rs. 3,00,000
∴ Trade Payables Turnover Ratio = Rs. 12,00,000 / Rs. 3,00,000 = 4 times

Example:
From the following information, calculate –
Trade receivables turnover ratio
Average collection period
Trade payable turnover ratio
Given:

Revenue from Operations	8,75,000
Creditors	90,000
Bills receivable	48,000
Bills payable	2,000
Purchases	4,20,000
Trade debtors	59,000

Solution:
Trade Receivables Turnover Ratio = Net Credit Revenue from operation / Average Trade Receivable
= Rs. 8, 75,000 / (Rs. 59,000 + Rs. 48,000) = 8.18 times
Average Collection Period = 365 / Trade Receivables Turnover Ratio = 365 / 8.18 = 45 days
Trade Payable Turnover Ratio = Purchases / Average Trade Payables
= Purchases / Creditors + Bills payable
= 4,20,000 / 90,000 + 52,000
= 4,20,000 / 1,42,000 = 2.96 times

Working Capital Turnover Ratio: It reflects relationship between revenue from operations and net assets (capital employed) in the business.

Working capital turnover ratio = Net Revenue from Operation / Working Capital

Profitability Ratios

Profitability ratios are calculated to analyse the earning capacity of the business which is the outcome of utilisation of resources employed in the business. There is a close relationship between the profit and the efficiency with which the resources employed in the business are utilised.

Gross Profit Ratio: Gross profit ratio as a percentage of revenue from operations is computed to have an idea about gross margin. It is computed as follows:

Gross Profit Ratio = Gross Profit / Net Revenue of Operations × 100
Example:

Following information is available for the year 2014-15, calculate gross profit ratio:

Revenue from Operations: Cash	25,000
Credit	75,000
Purchases: Cash	15,000
Credit	60,000
Carriage Inwards	2,000
Salaries	25,000
Decrease in Inventory	10,000
Return Outwards	2,000
Wages	5,000

Solution:

Revenue from Operations = Cash Revenue from Operations + Credit Revenue from Operation

= Rs.25, 000 + Rs.75, 000 = Rs. 1,00,000

Net Purchases = Cash Purchases + Credit Purchases – Return Outwards

 = Rs. 15,000 + Rs. 60,000 – Rs. 2,000 = Rs. 73,000

Cost of Revenue from = Purchases + (Opening Inventory – Closing Inventory) + operations Direct Expenses

= Purchases + Decrease in inventory + Direct Expenses

= Rs. 73,000 + Rs. 10,000 + (Rs. 2,000 + Rs. 5,000)

= Rs. 90,000

Gross Profit = Revenue from Operations – Cost of Revenue from Operation

= Rs. 1,00,000 – Rs. 90,000 = Rs. 10,000

Gross Profit Ratio = Gross Profit/Net Revenue from Operations × 100

= Rs.10,000/Rs.1,00,000 × 100 = 10%.

Operating Ratio: It is computed to analyse cost of operation in relation to revenue from operations.

It is calculated as follows:
Operating Ratio = (Cost of Revenue from Operations + Operating Expenses)/ Net Revenue from Operations × 100

Operating Profit Ratio: It is calculated to reveal operating margin. It may be computed directly or as a residual of operating ratio. It is calculated as under:

Operating Profit Ratio = Operating Profit/ Revenue from Operations × 100

Where,
Operating Profit = Revenue from Operations – Operating Cost

Example:
Given the following information:

Revenue from Operations	3,40,000
Cost of Revenue from Operations	1,20,000
Selling expenses	80,000
Administrative Expenses	40,000

Calculate Gross profit ratio and Operating ratio.

Solution:

Gross Profit = Revenue from Operations – Cost of Revenue from Operations

= Rs. 3,40,000 – Rs. 1,20,000

= Rs. 2,20,000

Gross Profit Ratio = Gross Profit / Revenue from operation × 100

= Rs. 2,20,000 / Rs. 3,40,000 × 100 = 64.71%

Operating Cost = Cost of Revenue from Operations + Selling Expenses + Administrative Expenses

= Rs. 1,20,000 + 80,000 + 40,000 = Rs. 2,40,000

Operating Ratio = Operating Cost / Net Revenue from Operations × 100

= Rs. 2,40,000 / Rs. 3,40,000 x 100 = 70.59%

Net Profit Ratio: It relates revenue from operations to net profit after operational as well as non-operational expenses and incomes. It is calculated as under:

Net Profit Ratio = Net profit / Revenue from Operations × 100

Return on Capital Employed or Investment: Capital employed means the long-term funds employed in the business and includes shareholders' funds, debentures and long-term loans.

Capital employed may be taken as the total of non-current assets and working capital. Profit refers to the Profit before Interest and Tax (PBIT) for computation of this ratio.

Thus, it is computed as follows:

Return on Investment (or Capital Employed) = Profit before Interest and Tax / Capital Employed × 100

Multiple Choice Questions

1. Interpretation of financial statements includes:
   - **A.** Criticisms and Analysis
   - **B.** Comparison and Trend Study
   - **C.** Drawing Conclusion
   - **D.** All the above

Answer: D

Explanation:

Interpretation of financial statements includes criticisms and analysis, comparison and trend study, drawing conclusions.

2. Horizontal Analysis is also known as:
   - **A.** Dynamic Analysis
   - **B.** Structural Analysis
   - **C.** Static Analysis
   - **D.** None of these

Answer: A

Explanation:

Horizontal Analysis is also known as dynamic analysis.

3. Vertical Analysis is also known as:
   - **A.** Static Analysis
   - **B.** Dynamic Analysis
   - **C.** Structural Analysis
   - **D.** None of these

Answer: A

Explanation:

Vertical Analysis is also known as static analysis.

4. Comparative Statements are also known as:
   - **A.** Dynamic Analysis
   - **B.** Horizontal Analysis
   - **C.** Vertical Analysis
   - **D.** External Analysis

Answer: B

Explanation:

Comparative Statements are also known as horizontal analysis.

5. Common-size Statement are also known as:

    A. Dynamic Analysis   **B.** Horizontal Analysis

    C. Vertical Analysis   **D.** External Analysis

Answer: C

Explanation:

Common-size Statement are also known as vertical analysis.

6. The most used tools for financial analysis are:

    A. Comparative Statements   **B.** Common-size Statement

    C. Accounting Ratios   **D.** All the above

Answer: D

Explanation:

The most used tools for financial analysis are comparative statements, common-size statement, accounting ratios.

7. The analysis of financial statement by a shareholder is an example of:

    A. External Analysis   **B.** Internal Analysis

    C. Vertical Analysis   **D.** Horizontal Analysis

Answer: A

Explanation:

The analysis of financial statements by a shareholder is an example of external analysis.

8. For calculating trend percentages any year is selected as:

    A. Current year   **B.** Previous year

    C. Base year   **D.** None of these

Answer: C

Explanation:

For calculating trend percentages any year is selected as base year.

9. Tools for comparison of financial statements are:

    A. Comparative Balance Sheet   **B.** Comparative Income Statement

    C. Common-size Statement   **D.** All the above

Answer: D

Explanation:

Tools for comparison of financial statements are Comparative Balance Sheet, Comparative Income Statement, Common-size Statement.

10. Trend ratios and trend percentage are used in:

    A. Dynamic analysis   **B.** Static analysis

    C. Horizontal analysis   **D.** Vertical Analysis

Answer: C

Explanation:

Trend ratios and trend percentage are used in Horizontal analysis.

11. Comparative Financial Statements show:

    A. Financial position of a concern   **B.** Earning capacity of a concern

    C. Both of them   **D.** None of these

Answer: C

Explanation:

Comparative Financial Statements show financial position of a concern and Earning capacity of a concern.

12. Which of these are not the method of financial statement analysis?

    A. Ratio Analysis   **B.** Comparative Analysis

    C. Trend Analysis   **D.** Capitalization Method

Answer: D

Explanation:

Capitalization Method is not the method of financial statement analysis. Capitalization is a method used to convert an estimate of a single year's income expectancy into an indication of value in one direct step.

13. Common-size financial statements are mostly prepared:

    A. In proportion   **B.** In percentage

    C. A and B both   **D.** None of these

Answer: B

Explanation:

Common-size financial statements are prepared in proportion and percentage.

14. A company's net sales are ₹ 15,00,000; cost of sales is ₹ 10,00,000 and indirect expenses are ₹ 3,00,000, the amount gross profit will be:

    A. ₹ 13,00,000   **B.** ₹ 5,00,000

    C. ₹ 2,00,000   **D.** ₹ 12,00,000

Answer: C

Explanation:

We can solve the question using the following steps:

To find the gross profit,

Gross Profit = Net Sales - (Cost of Sales + Indirect Expenses)

Substituting the given values,

Gross Profit = 15,00,000 – (10,00,000 + 3,00,000)

= 15,00,000 - 13,00,000
= ₹ 2,00,000

So, the amount gross profit will be ₹ 2,00,000.

15. Sales less Cost of goods sold is called:

    A. Operating Profit   **B.** Gross Profit

    C. Net Profit   **D.** Total Profit

Answer: B

Explanation:

Sales less Cost of goods sold is called gross profit.

16. In a common-size Balance Sheet, total equity and liabilities are assumed to be equal to:

    A. 1,000   **B.** 100

    C. 10   **D.** 1

Answer: B

Explanation:

In a common-size Balance Sheet, total equity and liabilities are assumed to be equal to 100.

17. Break-even point refers to that point where:

    A. Total Costs are more than Total Sales   **B.** Total Costs are less than Total Sales

    C. Total Costs are half of the Total Sales   **D.** Total Cost are equal to total sales

Answer: D

Explanation:

Break-even point refers to that total cost are equal to total sales.

18. Payment of Income Tax is considered as:

    A. Direct Expenses   **B.** Indirect Expenses

    C. Operating Expenses   **D.** None of these

Answer: B

Explanation:

Payment of income tax is considered as indirect expenses.

19. Vertical Analysis is also known as:

    A. Fluctuation Analysis   **B.** Static Analysis

    C. Horizontal Analysis   **D.** None of these

Answer: B

Explanation:

Vertical analysis is also known as static analysis.

20. Financial analysis is useful:

    A. For Investors   **B.** For Shareholders

    C. For Debenture holders   **D.** All the above

Answer: D

Explanation:

Financial analysis is useful For Investors, For Shareholders, For Debenture holders.

21. Analysis of financial statements involve:

    A. Trading A/c   **B.** Profit & Loss statement

    C. Balance Sheet   **D.** All the above

Answer: D

Explanation:

Analysis of financial statements involve Trading A/c, Profit & Loss statement, Balance Sheet.

22. Financial analysis is significant because it:

    A. Ignores qualitative aspect   **B.** Judges operational efficiency

    C. Suffers from the limitations of financial statements   **D.** It is affected by personal ability and bias of the analysis

Answer: B

Explanation:

Financial analysis is significant because it judges operational efficiency.

23. What is shown by the Income Statement?

    A. Accuracy of books of accounts   **B.** Profit or loss of a certain period

    C. Balance of Cash Book   **D.** None of these

Answer: B

Explanation:

Profit or loss for a certain period is shown by the Income Statement.

24. What is shown by Balance Sheet ?

    A. Accuracy of books of accounts   **B.** Profit or loss of a specific period

    C. Financial position on a specific date   **D.** None of the above

Answer: C

Explanation:

Financial position on a specific date is shown by Balance Sheet.

25. Which of the following is the purpose or objective of financial analysis ?

    A. To assess the current profitability of the firm   **B.** To measure the solvency of the firm

    C. To assess the short-term and long-term liquidity position of the firm   **D.** All the above

Answer: D

Explanation:

To assess the current profitability of the firm, to measure the solvency of the firm and to assess the short-term and long-term liquidity position of the firm are the purpose or objective of financial analysis.

26. Out of the following which parties are interested in financial statements?

    A. Managers   **B.** Financial Institutions

    C. Creditors   **D.** All the these

Answer: D

Explanation:

Managers, Financial Institutions, Creditors parties are interested in financial statements.

27. Which of the following is not a limitations of financial statement analysis?

    A. To measure the financial strength   **B.** Affected by window-dressing

    C. Do not reflect changes in price level   **D.** Lack of Qualitative Analysis

Answer: A

Explanation:

To measure the financial strength is not a limitations of financial statement analysis.

28. Break-even Analysis shows:

    A. Relationship between cost and sales   **B.** Relationship between production and purchases

    C. Relationship between cost and revenue   **D.** None of these

Answer: A

Explanation:

Break-even Analysis shows Relationship between cost and sales.

29. Which of the following shows the actual financial position of enterprise?

    A. Fund Flow   **B.** Balance Sheet

    C. P & L A/c   **D.** Ratio Analysis

Answer: B

Explanation:

Balance Sheet shows the actual financial position of enterprise.

30. The financial statements of a business enterprise include:

    A. Balance Sheet   **B.** Profit & Loss Account

    C. Cash Flow Statement   **D.** All the above

Answer: D

Explanation:

The financial statements of a business enterprise include Balance Sheet, Profit & Loss Account, Cash Flow Statement.

Chapter- 4   Cash Flow Statement

Introduction

There is also a third important financial statement known as Cash flow statement, which shows inflows and outflows of the cash and cash equivalents. This statement is usually prepared by companies which comes as a tool in the hands of users of financial information to know about the sources and uses of cash and cash equivalents of an enterprise over a period of time from various activities of an enterprise. It has gained substantial importance in the last decade because of its practical utility to the users of financial information.

Financial Statement of companies are prepared following the accounting standards prescribed in the companies Act, 2013. Accounting Standards are notified under section 133 of the Companies Act, 2013 vide Accounting Standards Rules, 2006 and are mandatory in nature. Companies Act, 2013 also specifies that if the accounting standards are not followed, financial statements will not be true and fair, which is a quality of financial statement. Financial Statements are defined in Companies Act, 2013 (Section 2 (40)] and include Cash Flow Statement prepared in accordance with Accounting Standard- 3 (AS-3)- Cash Flow Statement.

A cash flow statement provides information about the historical changes in cash and cash equivalents of an enterprise by classifying cash flows into operating, investing and financing activities. It requires that an enterprise should prepare a cash flow statement and should present it for each accounting period for which financial statements are presented. This chapter discusses this technique and explains the method of preparing a cash flow statement for an accounting period.

Objectives of Cash Flow Statement

A Cash flow statement shows inflow and outflow of cash and cash equivalents from various activities of a company during a specific period. The primary objective of cash flow statement is to provide useful information about cash flows (inflows and outflows) of an enterprise during a particular period under various heads, i.e., operating activities, investing activities and financing activities.

This information is useful in providing users of financial statements with a basis to assess the ability of the enterprise to generate cash and cash equivalents and the needs of the enterprise to utilise those cash flows. The economic decisions that are taken by users require an evaluation of the ability of an enterprise to generate cash and cash equivalents and the timing and certainty of their generation.

Benefits of Cash Flow Statement
Cash flow statement provides the following benefits:
- A cash flow statement when used along with other financial statements provides information that enables users to evaluate changes in net assets of an enterprise, its financial structure (including its liquidity and solvency) and its ability to affect the amounts and timings of cash flows in order to adapt to changing circumstances and opportunities.
- Cash flow information is useful in assessing the ability of the enterprise to generate cash and cash equivalents and enables users to develop models to assess and compare the present value of the future cash flows of different enterprises.
- It also enhances the comparability of the reporting of operating performance by different enterprises because it eliminates the effects of using different accounting treatments for the same transactions and events.
- It also helps in balancing its cash inflow and cash outflow, keeping in response to changing conditions. It is also helpful in checking the accuracy of past assessments of future cash flows and in examining the relationship between profitability and net cash flow and the impact of changing prices.

Cash and Cash Equivalents
As stated earlier, a cash flow statement shows inflows and outflows of cash and cash equivalents from various activities of an enterprise during a particular period. As per AS-3, 'Cash' comprises cash in hand and demand deposits with banks, and 'Cash equivalents' means short-term highly liquid investments that are readily convertible into known amounts of cash, and which are subject to an insignificant risk of changes in value. An investment normally qualifies as cash equivalents only when it has a short maturity, of say, three months or less from the date of acquisition. Investments in shares are excluded from cash equivalents unless they are in substantial cash equivalents. For example, preference shares of a company acquired shortly before their specific redemption date, provided there is only insignificant risk of failure of the company to repay the amount at maturity. Similarly, short-term marketable securities which can be readily converted into cash are treated as cash equivalents and is liquidable immediately without considerable change in value.

Cash Flows

'Cash Flows' implies movement of cash in and out due to some non-cash items. Receipt of cash from a non-cash item is termed as cash inflow while cash payment in respect of such items as cash outflow. For example, purchase of machinery by paying cash is cash outflow while sale proceeds received from sale of machinery is cash inflow. Other examples of cash flows include collection of cash from trade receivables, payment to trade payables, payment to employees, receipt of dividend, interest payments, etc. Cash management includes the investment of excess cash in cash equivalents. Hence, purchase of marketable securities or short-term investment which constitutes cash equivalents is not considered while preparing cash flow statement.

Classification of Activities for the Preparation of Cash Flow Statement

You know that various activities of an enterprise result in cash flows (inflows or receipts and outflows or payments) which is the subject matter of a cash flow statement. As per AS-3, these activities are to be classified into three categories:
(1) Operating
(2) Investing
(3) Financing activities to show separately the cash flows generated (or used) by (in) these activities.
This helps the users of cash flow statements to assess the impact of these activities on the financial position of an enterprise and on its cash and cash equivalents.

Cash from Operating Activities

Operating activities are the activities that constitute the primary or main activities of an enterprise. For example, for a company manufacturing garments, operating activities are procurement of raw material, incurrence of manufacturing expenses, sale of garments, etc. These are the principal revenue generating activities (or the main activities) of the enterprise and these activities are not investing or financing activities. The amount of cash from operations indicates the internal solvency level of the company and is regarded as the key indicator of the extent to which the operations of the enterprise have generated sufficient cash flows to maintain the operating capability of the enterprise, paying dividends, making of new investments, and repaying of loans without recourse to external source of financing.

Cash flows from operating activities are primarily derived from the main activities of the enterprise. They generally result from transactions and other events that enter the determination of net profit or loss. Examples of cash flows from operating activities are:

Cash Inflows from operating activities

- Cash receipts from sale of goods and the rendering of services.
- Cash receipts from royalties, fees, commissions and other revenues.

Cash Outflows from operating activities

- Cash payments to suppliers for goods and services.
- Cash payments to and on behalf of the employees.
- Cash payments to an insurance enterprise for premiums and claims, annuities, and other policy benefits.
- Cash payments of income taxes unless they can be specifically identified with financing and investing activities.

The net position is shown in case of operating cash flows

An enterprise may hold securities and loans for dealing or for trading purposes. In either case they represent Inventory specifically held for resale. Therefore, cash flows arising from the purchase and sale of dealing or trading securities are classified as operating activities. Similarly, cash advances and loans made by financial enterprises are usually classified as operating activities since they relate to the main activity of that enterprise.

Cash from Investing Activities

As per AS-3, investing activities are the acquisition and disposal of long-term assets and other investments not included in cash equivalents. Investing activities relate to purchase and sale of long-term assets or fixed assets such as machinery, furniture, land and building, etc. Transactions related to long term investment are also investing activities.

Separate disclosure of cash flows from investing activities is important because they represent the extent to which expenditures have been made for resources intended to generate future income and cash flows. Examples of cash flows arising from investing activities are:

Cash Outflows from investing activities

- Cash payments to acquire fixed assets including intangibles and capitalized research and development.

- Cash payments to acquire shares, warrants or debt instruments of other enterprises other than the instruments those held for trading purposes.
- Cash advances and loans made to third party (other than advances and loans made by a financial enterprise wherein it is operating activities).

Cash Inflows from Investing Activities
- Cash receipt from disposal of fixed assets including intangibles.
- Cash receipt from the repayment of advances or loans made to third parties (except in case of financial enterprise).
- Cash receipt from disposal of shares, warrants or debt instruments of other enterprises except those held for trading purposes.
- Interest received in cash from loans and advances.
- Dividend received from investments in other enterprises.

Cash from Financing Activities
As the name suggests, financing activities relate to long-term funds or capital of an enterprise, e.g., cash proceeds from issue of equity shares, debentures, raising long-term bank loans, repayment of bank loan, etc. As per AS-3, financing activities are activities that result in changes in the size and composition of the owners' capital (including preference share capital in case of a company) and borrowings of the enterprise. Separate disclosure of cash flows arising from financing activities is important because it is useful in predicting claims on future cash flows by providers of funds (both capital and borrowings) to the enterprise. Examples of financing activities are:

Cash Inflows from financing activities
- Cash proceeds from issuing shares (equity or/and preference).
- Cash proceeds from issuing debentures, loans, bonds and other short/ long-term borrowings.

Cash Outflows from financing activities
- Cash repayments of amounts borrowed.
- Interest paid on debentures and long-term loans and advances.
- Dividends paid on equity and preference capital.

It is important to mention here that a transaction may include cash flows that are classified differently. For example, when the instalment paid in respect of a fixed asset acquired on deferred payment basis includes both interest and loan, the interest element is classified under financing activities and the loan element is classified under investing activities. Moreover, same activity may be classified differently for different enterprises. For example, purchase of shares is an operating activity for a share brokerage firm while it is investing activity in case of other enterprises.

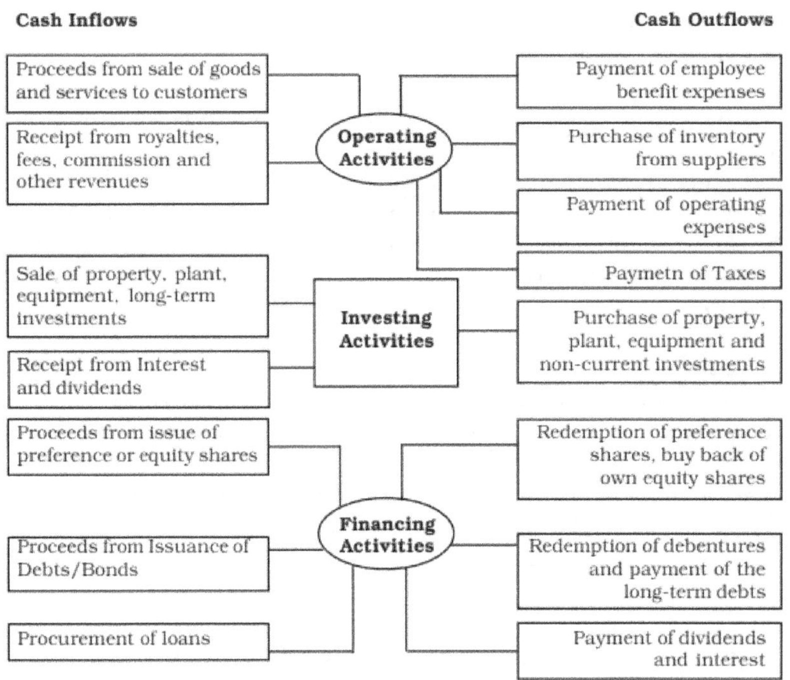

Extraordinary items

Extraordinary items are not the regular phenomenon, e.g., loss due to theft or earthquake or flood. Extraordinary items are non-recurring in nature and hence cash flows associated with extraordinary items should be classified and disclosed separately as arising from operating, investing or financing activities. This is done to enable users to understand their nature and effect on the present and future cash flows of an enterprise.

Interest and Dividend

In the case of a financial enterprise (whose main business is lending and borrowing), interest paid, interest received and dividend received are classified as operating activities while dividend paid is a financing activity.

In the case of a non-financial enterprise, as per AS-3, it is considered more appropriate that payment of interest and dividends are classified as financing activities whereas receipt of interest and dividends are classified as investing activities.

Taxes on Income and Gains

Taxes may be income tax (tax on normal profit), capital gains tax (tax on capital profits), dividend tax (tax on the amount distributed as dividend to shareholders). AS-3 requires that cash flows arising from taxes on income should be separately disclosed and should be classified as cash flows from operating activities unless they can be specifically identified with financing and investing activities. This clearly implies that:

* tax on operating profit should be classified as operating cash flows.
* dividend tax, i.e., tax paid on dividend should be classified as financing activity along with dividend paid.
* Capital gains tax paid on sale of fixed assets should be classified under investing activities.

Non-cash Transactions

As per AS-3, investing and financing transactions that do not require the use of cash or cash equivalents should be excluded from a cash flow statement. Examples of such transactions are - acquisition of machinery by issue of equity shares or redemption of debentures by issue of equity shares. Such transactions should be disclosed elsewhere in the financial statements in a way that provide all the relevant information about these investing and financing activities. Hence, assets acquired by issue of shares are not disclosed in cash flow statement due to non-cash nature of the transaction. With these three classifications, Cash Flow Statement is shown.

Cash Flow Statement
(Main heads only)

(A) Cash flows from operating activities	xxx
(B) Cash flows from investing activities	xxx
(C) Cash flows from financing activities	xxx
Net increase (decrease) in cash and cash equivalents (A + B + C)	xxx
+ Cash and cash equivalents at the beginning	xxx
= Cash and cash equivalents at the end	xxxx

Ascertaining Cash Flow from Operating Activities

Operating activities are the main source of revenue and expenditure in an enterprise. Therefore, the ascertainment of cash flows from operating activities needs special attention. As per AS-3, an enterprise should report cash flows from operating activities either by using:

* Direct method whereby major classes of gross cash receipts and gross cash payments are disclosed; or
* Indirect method whereby net profit or loss is duly adjusted for the effects of (1) transactions of a non-cash nature, (2) any deferrals or accruals of past/future operating cash receipts, and (3) items of income or expenses associated with investing or financing cash flows. It is important to mention here that under indirect method, the starting point is net profit/loss before taxation and extra ordinary items as per Statement of Profit and Loss of the enterprise. Then this amount is for non-cash items, etc., adjusted for ascertaining cash flows from operating activities.

Accordingly, cash flow from operating activities can be determined using either the Direct method or the Indirect method. The direct method provides information which is useful in estimating future cash flows. But such information is not available under the indirect method. However, in practice, indirect methods are mostly used by the companies for arriving at the net cash flow from operating activities. The Chapter deals with preparing cash flow statements using indirect method.

Proposed Dividend

As per AS-4, Contingencies and Events Occurring after the Balance Sheet Date, Proposed dividend is shown in the Notes to Accounts. It will be shown as contingent liability since it becomes a liability after it is declared (approved) by the shareholders. It will be accounted for in the books of account after it is declared (approved) by the shareholders in the Annual General Meeting. Since, previous year's Proposed Dividend will be declared (approved) in the current year; the previous year's Proposed Dividend will be accounted as dividend payable. Also, a declared dividend is paid within 30 days of its declaration; therefore, it will be paid within the same financial year.

Briefly, the proposed dividend of the previous year after declaration (approved) by the shareholders will be debited to surplus i.e., Balance in Statement of Profit and Loss. While preparing the cash flow statement, previous year's proposed dividend will be added to Act Profit under operating activities and will be shown under financial activity.

Indirect Method

The indirect method of ascertaining cash flow from operating activities begins with the amount of net profit/loss. This is so because a statement of profit and loss incorporates the effects of all operating activities of an enterprise. However, the Statement of Profit and Loss is prepared on an accrual basis (and not on cash basis). Moreover, it also includes certain non-operating items such as interest paid, profit/loss on sale of fixed assets, etc.) and non-cash items (such as depreciation, goodwill written-off, dividend declared, etc. Therefore, it becomes necessary to adjust the amount of net profit/loss as shown by the Statement of Profit and Loss for arriving at cash flows from operating activities. Let us look at the example:

Statement of Profit and Loss Account for the year ended March 31, 2017

Particulars	Note	Figures in (Rs.)
i)Revenue from Operations		1,00,000
ii)Other Income	1	2,000
iii) Total Revenues (i+ii)		1,02,000
iv)Expenses		
Cost of Materials Consumed		30,000
Purchases of stock-in-trade		10,000
Employees Benefits Expenses		10,000
Finance Costs		5,000
Depreciation		12,000
Other Expenses		72,000
v) Profit before Tax (iii- iv)		30,000

The above Statement of Profit and Loss shows the amount of net profit of Rs. 30,000. This has to be adjusted for arriving cash flows from operating activities. Let us take various items one by one.

- Depreciation is a non-cash item and hence, Rs. 5,000 charged as depreciation does not result in any cash flow. Therefore, this amount must be added back to the net profit.
- Finance costs of Rs. 5,000 is a cash outflow on account of financing activity. Therefore, this amount must also be added back to net profit while calculating cash flows from operating activities. This amount of finance cost will be shown as an outflow under the head of financing activities.
- Other income includes profit on sale of land: It is cash inflow from investing activity. Hence, this amount must be deducted from the amount of net profit while calculating cash flows from operating activities.

The above example gives you an idea as to how various adjustments are made in the amount of net profit/loss. Other important adjustments relate to changes in working capital which are necessary (i.e., items of current assets and current liabilities) to convert net profit/loss which is based on accrual basis into cash flows from operating activities. Therefore, the increase in current assets and decrease in current liabilities are deducted from the operating profit, and the decrease in current assets and increase in current liabilities are added to the operating profit so as to arrive at the exact amount of net cash flow from operating activities. As per AS-3, under indirect method, net cash flow from operating activities is determined by adjusting net profit or loss for the effect of:

- Non-cash items such as depreciation, goodwill written-off, provisions, deferred taxes, etc., which are to be added back.
- All other items for which the cash effects are investing or financing cash flows. The treatment of such items depends upon their nature. All investing and financing incomes are to be deducted from the amount of net profits while all such expenses

are to be added back. For example, finance cost which is a financing cash outflow is to be added back while other income such as interest received which is investing cash inflow is to be deducted from the amount of net profit. Dividend declared is a financial activity and is therefore added back to net profit and shown as out flow under financial activity.

- Changes in current assets and liabilities during the period. Increase in current assets and decrease in current liabilities are to be deducted while increase in current liabilities and decrease in current assets are to be added up.

Cash Flows from Operating Activities (Indirect Method)	
Net Profit/Loss before Tax and Extraordinary Items	XXX
+ Deductions already made in Statement of Profit and Loss on account of Non-cash items such as Depreciation, Goodwill to be Written-off.	XXX
+ Deductions already made in Statement of Profit and Loss on Account of Non-operating items such as Interest.	XXX
− Additions (incomes) made in Statement of Profit and Loss on Account of Non-operating items such as Dividend received, Profit on sale of Fixed Assets.	XXX
Operating Profit before Working Capital changes	
Add : in case of increase in current assets (other than cash and cash	XXX
equivalent) and decrease in current liabilities.	
Less : in case of decrease in current assets (other than cash and cash	XXX
equivalent) and decrease in current liabilities.	
Cash Flows from Operation Activities before Tax and Extraordinary items	XXX
− Income Tax Paid	XXX
+/ Effects of Extraordinary Items	XXX
Net Cash from Operating Activities	**XXX**

As stated earlier, while working out the cash flow from operating activities, the starting point is the 'Net profit before tax and extraordinary items' and not the 'Net profit as per Statement of Profit and Loss'. Income tax paid is deducted as the last item to arrive at the net cash flow from operating activities.

Illustration

Using the data given in Illustration 1, calculate cash flows from operating activities using indirect method.

Solution:

Cash Flows from Operating Activities

Particulars	(Rs.)
(Net Profit before Taxation and Extraordinary Items (Note 1) Adjustments for- + Depreciation	42,000 20,000
= Operating Profit before working capital changes	62,000
- Increase in Trade Receivables	(3,000)
- Increase in Inventories	(5,000)
- Increase in Prepaid Insurance	(500)
- Decrease in Trade Payables	(2,000)
+ Increase in Outstanding Employees Benefits Expenses	+1,000
= Cash generated from Operations	52,500
− Income tax paid	(11,000)
= Net cash from Operating Activities	**41, 500**

You will notice that the amount of cash flows from operating activities are the same whether we use direct method or indirect method for its calculation.

Working Notes:

The net profit before taxation and extraordinary items has been worked out as under:

Net Profit	= Rs. 32,000
+ Income Tax	= Rs. 10,000
= Net Profit before Tax and Extraordinary Items	= Rs. 42,000

The details of items leading inflows and outflows from investing and financing activities have already been outlined. While preparing the cash flow statement, all major items of gross cash receipts, gross cash payments, and net cash flows from investing and financing activities must be shown separately under the headings 'Cash Flow from Investing Activities' and 'Cash Flow from Financing Activities' respectively.'

The ascertainment of net cash flows from investing and financing activities have been briefly dealt with in Illustrations 5 and 6.

Illustration

WellPoint Ltd. has given you the following information:

Machinery as on April 01, 2016	Rs. 50,000
Machinery as on March 31, 2017	Rs. 60,000
Accumulated Depreciation on April 01, 2016	Rs. 25,000
Accumulated Depreciation on March 31, " 2017)	Rs. 15,000

During the year, a Machine costing Rs. 25,000 with an Accumulated Depreciation of Rs. 15,000 was sold for Rs. 13,000.
Calculate cash flow from Investing Activities based on the above information.

Solution:

Cash Flows from Investing Activities

Sale of Machinery	Rs. 13,000
Purchase of Machinery	(35,000)
Net cash used in Investing Activities	(22,000)

Working Notes:

Machinery Account

Particulars	J.F.	Amount (Rs.)	Particulars	J.F.	Amount (Rs.)
Balance b/d Statement of Profit and Loss		50,000	Cash (proceeds from sale of machine)		13,000
(profit on sale of machine) Cash (balancing figure: new		3,000	Accumulated		
machinery purchased)		35,000	Depreciation		15,000
		88,000	Balance c/d		60,000
					88,000

Accumulated Depreciation Account

Particulars	J.F.	Amount (Rs.)	Particulars	J.F.	Amount (Rs.)
Machinery		15,000	Balance b/d		25,000
Balance c/d		15,000	Statement of Profit and Loss (Depreciation provided during the year)		5,000
		30,000			30,000

Preparation of Cash Flow Statement

As stated earlier cash flow statement provides information about change in the position of Cash and Cash Equivalents of an enterprise, over an accounting period. The activities contributing to this change are classified into operating, investing and financing. The methodology of working out the net cash flow (or use) from all the three activities for an accounting period has been explained in details and a brief format of Cash Flow Statement has also been given in Exhibit 6.2. However, while preparing a cash flow statement, full details of inflows and outflows are given under these heads including the net cash flow (or use). The aggregate of the net 'cash flows (or use) is worked out and is shown as 'Net Increase/Decrease in cash and Cash Equivalents' to which the amount of 'cash and cash equivalent at the beginning' is added and thus the amount of 'cash and cash equivalents at the end' is arrived at as shown in Exhibit 6.2. This figure will be the same as the total amount of cash in hand, cash at bank and cash equivalents (if any) given in the balance sheet (see Illustrations 7 to 10). Another point that needs to be noted is that when cash flows from operating activities are worked out by an indirect method and shown as such in the cash flow statement, the statement itself is termed as 'Indirect method cash flow statement'. Thus, the Cash flow statements prepared in Illustrations 7,8 and 9 fall under this category as the cash flows from operating activities have been worked out by indirect method. Similarly, if the cash flows from operating activities are worked by direct method while preparing the cash flow statement, it will be termed as 'direct method Cash Flow Statement'. Illustration 10 shows both types of Cash Flow Statement. However, unless it is specified clearly as to which method is to be used, the cash flow statement may preferably be prepared by an indirect method as is done by most companies in practice.

Illustration

From the following information, prepare Cash Flow Statement for Pioneer Ltd.
Balance Sheet of Pioneer Ltd., as on March 31, 2017

Particulars		Amount (Rs.)	Amount (Rs.)
I. **Equity and Liabilities**			
1. Shareholders' Funds			
a) Share capital	1	7,00,000	5,00,000
b) Reserve and surplus	2	4,20,000	2,50,000
2. Non-current Liabilities			
Long-term borrowings: 10% Bank Load		50,000	1,00,000
3. Current Liabilities			
a) Trade Payables		45,000	50,000
b) Other current liabilities: outstanding rent		7,000	5,000
c) Short-term provisions		50,000	30,000
		12,72,000	**9,35,000**
II. Assets			
1. Non-current assets			
a) Fixed assets			
i) Tangible assets		5,00,000	5,00,000
ii) Intangible assets		95,000	1,00,000
b) Non-current investments		1,00,000	-
2. Current assets			
a) Inventories		1,30,000	50,000
b) Trade receivables		1,20,000	80,000
c) Cash and cash equivalents		3.27.000	2,05,000
Total		**12,72,000**	**9,35,000**

Multiple Choice Questions

1. The cash flow statement analysis is described in terms of which of the following activities?

    A. Operating activities   **B.** Financing activities

    C. Investing activities   **D.** All of the above

Answer: D

Explanation:

The cash flow statement analysis is described in terms of operating activities, financing activities and investing activities.

2. In the cash flow statement if the company invests more in fixed assets and short-term financial investments, it will result to:

    A. Decreased cash   **B.** Increased cash

    C. Increased equity   **D.** Increased liability

Answer: A

Explanation:

The fixed assets include furniture, land machinery, and building. Investing in such fixed assets and investing in short-term financial investments leads to decreased cash.

3. Which of the following are regarded as financial activities in the cash flow?

    A. The interest that is paid   **B.** The issue of preference share

    C. The redemption of the preference share   **D.** All of the above

Answer: D

Explanation:

The interest that is paid, the issue of preference share and the redemption of the preference share are regarded as financial activities in the cash flow.

4. An activity that falls under operating activity in the cash flow statement is:

- **A.** The sales of the fixed asset
- **B.** The interest that is paid on term deposits by a bank
- **C.** The purchase of the own debenture
- **D.** The sewing of equity share capital

Answer: B

Explanation:

Operational activities are the activities required to carry out a company's operations. The activities include interest paid to terms deposited by banks, the salary of the employees, etc.

5. The cash flow statement will define the cash flow concerning which of the following?

- **A.** The operating and non-operating flows
- **B.** The outflow and inflow
- **C.** The investing and non-operating floors
- **D.** The investing, operating, and financing activities

Answer: D

Explanation:

The definition of the cash flow statement scribes the flow of cash in terms of operating activities, investing activities, and financing activities.

6. Who will be interested in the cash flow statements of a company?

- **A.** The directors of the company
- **B.** The shareholders of the company
- **C.** The potential investors of the company
- **D.** All of the above

Answer: D

Explanation:

They will be interested in the cash flow statement to ensure the company doesn't trade while insolvent; the potential investors and shareholders will be interested in the cash flow statement to know its financial condition.

7. What does the cash flow statement intend to do?

- **A.** The future cash flows and borrowing could be predicted
- **B.** Different companies can be easily compared with each other
- **C.** Provide formation regarding a company's solvency, liquidity, and financial stability
- **D.** All of the above

Answer: D

Explanation:

The cash flow statement tells us many things about a company like it's like the future cash flow. The performance of the two companies can be analysed by comparing the cash flow statements.

8. The company which issues bonds and stocks to raise funds will result to:

- **A.** Increase in cash
- **B.** decrease in cash
- **C.** increase in the liabilities
- **D.** increase in the equity

Answer: A

Explanation:

When more bonds and stocks are issued, the fit gain from these activities will increase cash in the organisation. This cash can be used to carry out other activities and operations in the company.

9. The activity which is recorded as investing activity in cash flow is:

- **A.** Sale of investment by non-financial enterprise
- **B.** Issuing a debenture
- **C.** Paying back a loan
- **D.** The raw material purchased with cash

Answer: A

Explanation:

The activities which fall under the investing activities of the cash flow statement are the collection of loans, proceeds of insurance settlements and the sale of investment instruments like bonds and stocks.

10. The financial statements will include which of the following entities?

- **A.** The balance sheet and the income statement
- **B.** The statement regarding the equity of shareholders
- **C.** The statements of the cash flow
- **D.** All of the above

Answer: D

There are five types of financial statements, which include: the statement of change in equity, the cash flow statement, the income statement, the statement regarding equity of the cash holder and the statement of the financial position.

11. Will the purchase value of assets over IT serviceable life come under the following terms?
  A. appreciated assets
  B. appreciated liabilities
  C. depreciation
  D. appreciation

Answer: C

Explanation:
Calculating the cost of tangible assets over their useful life is accounted for by depreciation. Hence, the purchase value of assets over their serviceable life will come under depreciation.

12. Which of the following are the objectives of the cash flow statement?
  A. The cash basis of the accounting
  B. The credit basis of the accounting
  C. The accrual basis of the accounting
  D. None of the above

Answer: A

Explanation:
The cash flow statement provides data about the company's cash flow due to ongoing operations. Its main focus is the flow of cash aspect of the accounting and not the credit or the accrual aspect.

13. What of the following statements will be considered false?
  A. Cash flow statements are useful for forming policies.
  B. The external analysis can be performed with a cash flow statement.
  C. The cash flow can be estimated with the help of a cash flow statement.
  D. None of the above

Answer: D

Explanation:
The cash flow statement is of a lot of use. It helps estimate future cash flow, helps people outside the company for external analysis, and the directors of a company can form policies based on the cash flow statement.

14. The cash flow statement is also called:
  A. The statement for accounting for the variation in cash
  B. The statement of changes in financial position based on cash
  C. Both (A) and (B)
  D. None of the above

Answer: C

Explanation:
The cash flow statement describes the variation inflow of cash and describes the change in a financial position concerning cash.

15. The cash flow statement is prepared from which of the following?
  A. By making use of the balance sheet
  B. The profit and loss account are used
  C. Additional information
  D. All of the above

Answer: D

Explanation:
A lot of information about cash flow is required to prepare the cash flow statement. This includes information about profit and loss accounts for the balance sheet information and extra information.

16. Which of the following must be eliminated to calculate cash flow shown in the profit and loss account converted into receipts and payments?
  A. Non-cash expenses from the expenses which were incurred
  B. The non-cash revenue from the revenue which is earned
  C. Both (A) and (B)
  D. None of the above

Answer: C

Explanation: The profit and loss account contains the non-cash revenues and expenses as well. They need to be eliminated to calculate the cash flow of the operating activities shown in the profit and loss account.

17. How is the cash flow due to the sales calculated?
  A. opening debtors + sales + opening B/R – closing debtors – closing B/R
  B. cash collections + cash sales
  C. None of these
  D. Both (A) and (B)

Answer: D

Explanation:

The cash flow due to cells can be calculated by adding cash sales with cash collection. It can also be calculated by adding opening debtors and opening B/R and sales while subtracting closing debtors and closing B/R.

18. Which of the following come under investing activities in the cash flow?

    A. Sale of fixed assets   **B.** The interest that is received

    C. Dividend received   **D.** All of the above

Answer: D

Explanation:

The sale of fixed assets, interest received, and the dividend received all come under the investing activities of the cash flow.

19. Sale of Copyrights is concerned with______.

    A. Investing Activities   **B.** Operating Activities

    C. Both Operating Activities and Financing Activities   **D.** Financing Activities

Answer: A

Explanation:

Sale of Copyrights is concerned with Investing Activities.

20. Dividend Received is concerned with_______.

    A. Investing Activities   **B.** Operating Activities

    C. Financing Activities   **D.** Both Operating Activities and Financing Activities

Answer: A

Explanation:

Dividend Received is concerned with investing activities.

21. Refund of income tax is the part of:

    A. Operating activities in Cash Flow Statement   **B.** Financing Activities in Cash Flow Statement

    C. Investing Activities in Cash Flow Statement   **D.** All of the above

Answer: A

Explanation:

Refund of income tax is the part of operating activities in cash flow statement.

22. Rent received is classified under:

    A. Investing Activities   **B.** Operating Activities

    C. Cash and Cash Equivalents   **D.** Financing Activities

Answer: A

Explanation:

Rent received is classified under Investing Activities.

23. In indirect method, which is used to calculate the amount of net cash flow from operating activities:

    A. Net income figure from the income statement   **B.** Net loss figure from Profit & Loss

    C. Net Profit figure from Profit & Loss   **D.** All of the options

Answer: A

Explanation:

Net income figure from the income statement is used to calculate the amount of net cash flow from operating activities.

24. Which activities are the same for Computation of Direct and indirect method?

    A. Cash Flow from Financing Activities and Cash flow from Investment activities   **B.** Cash Flow from Operating Activities and Cash flow from Investment activities

    C. Cash Flow from Operating Activities and Cash flow from financial activities   **D.** All of the above

Answer: A

Explanation:

Cash Flow from Financing Activities and Cash flow from Investment activities are the same for Computation of Direct and indirect method.

25. The main difference in direct and indirect method is to calculate the:

    A.   Cash flow from operating activities
    B.   Cash Flow from Financing Activities
    C.   Cash Flow from Investing Activities
    D.   All of the options

Answer: A

Explanation:

The main difference in direct and indirect method is to calculate the Cash flow from operating activities.

26. Which is the Method for the preparation of cash flow statement?

    A.   Both Direct and Indirect
    B.   Direct Method
    C.   Indirect Method
    D.   Average Method

Answer: A

Explanation:

Both Direct and Indirect is the Method for the preparation of cash flow statement.

27. How many methods for the preparation of cash flow statement?

    A.   2
    B.   3
    C.   4
    D.   5

Answer: A

Explanation:

There are 2 ways to prepare a cash flow statement: the direct method and the indirect method: Direct method – Operating cash flows are presented as a list of ingoing and outgoing cash flows.

28. A cash flow statement is also prepared to determine the:

    A.   Liquidity position of the organization
    B.   Debt position of the organization
    C.   Net Profit position of the organization
    D.   Net Profit position of the organization

Answer: A

Explanation:

A cash flow statement is also prepared to determine the liquidity position of the organization.

29. The most important objective of cash flow statement is that helps to ascertain the and outflows of cash and from:

    A.   Cash equivalents
    B.   Gross inflows
    C.   Outflows of cash
    D.   All of these

Answer: D

Explanation:

The most important objective of cash flow statement is that helps to ascertain the and outflows of cash and from Gross inflows, Outflows of cash, Cash equivalents.

30. When Company repurchases shares, pays dividends or pays off debt, it records a:

    A.   Cash outflow
    B.   Cash inflow
    C.   Not related to cash
    D.   All of the options

Answer: A

Explanation:

Company repurchases shares, pays dividends or pays off debt, it records a Cash outflow.

www.ingramcontent.com/pod-product-compliance
Lightning Source LLC
LaVergne TN
LVHW080549200726
843510LV00008B/1058